An extre... ...red
the boar...

Aquiline nos... ...to look down on people—finely chiseled aristocratic features, thick jet-black hair with a natural wave, extraordinary eyes the color of blue flame: immediate impact that would linger for a long time. He stood well over six feet, and was very elegantly dressed. A tailor's dream. So sophisticated was his appearance it held them all speechless for a while.

But none was more transfixed than Cate.

Time collapsed. How vivid was memory! How powerful was the past!

For a fleeting moment she felt her breathing had stopped. Then, as air came back into her lungs, she knew such fright she thought she had actually fainted while still remaining conscious. Her whole body was shaking, her mind sliding out of kilter.

This is it, she thought.

The heavens had shifted. She knew he had taken her in at once.

Lord Julian Ashton Carlisle, Fifth Baron Wyndham.

The father of her child.

MARGARET WAY

The English Lord's Secret Son

HARLEQUIN®
entertain, enrich, inspire™

Recycling programs
for this product may
not exist in your area.

ISBN-13: 978-0-373-74204-2

THE ENGLISH LORD'S SECRET SON

First North American Publication 2012

Margaret Way, a definite Leo, was born and raised in the subtropical river city of Brisbane, capital of the Sunshine State of Queensland, Australia. A Conservatorium-trained pianist, teacher, accompanist and vocal coach, she found her musical career came to an unexpected end when she took up writing—initially as a fun thing to do. She currently lives in a harborside apartment at beautiful Raby Bay, a thirty-minute drive from the state capital, where she loves dining *al fresco* on her plant-filled balcony, overlooking a translucent green marina filled with all manner of pleasure craft: from motor cruisers costing millions of dollars, and big, graceful yachts with carved masts standing tall against the cloudless blue sky, to little bay runabouts. No one and nothing is in a mad rush, and she finds the laid-back village atmosphere very conducive to her writing. With well over one hundred books to her credit, she still believes her best is yet to come.

Books by Margaret Way

ARGENTINIAN IN THE OUTBACK*
THE CATTLE KING'S BRIDE*
MASTER OF THE OUTBACK
IN THE AUSTRALIAN BILLIONAIRE'S ARMS
HER OUTBACK COMMANDER
AUSTRALIA'S MAVERICK MILLIONAIRE

*The Langdon Dynasty duet

Other titles by this author available in ebook format.

CHAPTER ONE

SEVEN-YEAR-OLD Jules slapped a fist into his palm as Cate nosed the Beemer into the parking space vacated by a runabout so compact it could fit into the owner's pocket.

"Good one, Mum," he whooped.

"Talk about perfect timing!" Cate Hamilton had come to rely on her parking skills. At times like this they proved invaluable.

"That was ace!"

Ace had taken over from the battered *awesome*. Jules always liked to keep a pace ahead.

"Noah really looks up to you, Mum." It was a source of pride to him. Noah, his best friend, was seriously impressed by Cate's driving. Noah's mother, a nice lady, had the really scary knack of either side swiping vehicles or on occasions reversing into them. She should have had a number plate bearing the warning: WATCH OUT. There were always scrapes and dents on their silver Volvo. Repairs were carried out. Back to Square One. It was a pattern pretty well set. Noah said his mother didn't know *how* to explain it. His father had a hard time understanding it as well.

So did Cate. She often had coffee with Noah's mother, who was a bright, intelligent woman, right on the ball, apart from her driving habits. She switched off the ignition, eyeing the busy road. At this time of the morning there were cars everywhere, causing a worrying amount of chaos. There didn't appear to be any order on the part of the drivers. She had even begun to question the safety of the pedestrian crossing. People appeared to be in such a desperate hurry these days. Where were they going? What was so important every nanosecond counted? Surely nothing could be more important than the safety of a child? The difficulty was, parking spots were at a premium for the junior school. Small children, even big children, didn't leg it to school these days. They didn't even bus it. They were driven to and fro by their parents. Different times, worrying times. Or maybe that perception was a beat up by a media who seized on anything when there was a dearth of stories.

A recent coverage featured an attempted snatching of a thirteen-year-old schoolgirl. Even the police had been sucked in for a while until a child psychologist in their ranks pointed out thirteen-year-old girls were known to have a burgeoning need for attention. Some were more demanding and more inventive than others. That particular young lady had a future writing fiction.

Cate glanced at her son's glowing face. The most beautiful face in the whole wide world to her. Not only beautiful, Jules was *smart*, really smart. Her one and only child. Pure and innocent. Her sun, moon and stars. Cate relished the moment of real joy, lifting a hand to acknowledge a departing driver, another mother, who fluttered curling, separated fingers in response.

It was a beautiful day, so bright and full of promise. A great time to be alive. Scent of trees. Scent of flowers, the heat amplifying the myriad scents to incense. Tangy taste of salt off Sydney Harbour. The Harbour, the most beautiful natural harbour in the world, made a splendid contribution to Sydney's scenic beauty. No wonder Sydney was regularly featured as one of the world's most beautiful and liveable cities. Few cities could boast such a glorious environment, a dazzling blue and gold world, with hundreds of bays and beaches of white sands, magical coves and waterways for its citizens to enjoy. To Sydneysiders it was a privilege to live within easy distance of the sparkling Pacific Ocean. Even the trip to school was a heart-lifting experience.

The great jacaranda trees that lined Kingsley Avenue on both sides were in full bloom. She recalled as a student it was a superstition among them that if a jacaranda blossom fell on one's head, one would pass one's exams. A fanciful notion and, like all fanciful notions, not one to count on. Nothing in life was as simple as that. Blossoms fell indiscriminately on heads all the time. This morning there were circular lavender carpets around the trunks, with spent blossoms fanning out across the pavement and the road.

Cate turned off the ignition. Only a short time to go now before term was over. The long Christmas vacation lay ahead.

Christmas.

Out of the blue her mind gave way to memories. She could never predict when they would invade her consciousness, frame by frame, unstoppable now, near obscuring her vision. A moment before she had been celebrating life. Now was not the time to allow dark thoughts to kick in. Yet inexorably she found herself going back in time to a place she knew from bitter experience was no place to go. Christmas across the world where it snowed instead of rained mauve blossom; where snow blanketed roofs and gardens, and frosted the trees, their skeletal branches outlined in white. For all the frigid air it was a world transformed. A fairy land.

Another time. Another place…

* * *

She had turned eighteen, an innocent at large, at the happiest, most exciting time of her young life, when the road ahead offered nothing but promise. She had thought at the time her guardian angel had to be watching over her, because it was then she fell helplessly, hopelessly, in love. The miracle of Destiny. She had revelled in the magic for long dreamlike months before all her happiness had been cruelly snatched away.

Overnight.

How *was* one supposed to respond to having one's heart broken? Not just broken, *trampled* on with feet that came down hard. What had been required of her was to absorb the terrible loss and disappear like a puff of smoke.

A Housman poem had run continuously in her head for years.

Give crowns and pounds and guineas
But not your heart away.

She had come to think of it as her theme song. She had given her heart away and given it in vain. She had learned a hard lesson—were there any better?—there were never guarantees when two people fell in love. What was love anyway between a man and a woman? A period of mesmerising madness? A period of lust, a desperation to assuage a physical hunger, without a single thought as to looking deeper for longer-lasting qualities? Just how many people were blessed with the sort of love that endured? Love for *life*. Was that too much to expect given the fickleness and limited attention span of human nature? Far too many suffered the sort of love that vanished as suddenly as it arrived. A case of love running out.

Or in my case, without warning, a changing course.

These days she was back to loving Christmas, indeed the whole festive season. The arrival of Jules had miraculously put her world to rights. She could see the big picture as she had never done before. From the instant he had been placed on her breast, he had become the most important person in the world to her. No love like a mother's love. No passion as strong. His impact on her very existence was profound. She no longer focused on herself and her pain. She had a *son* to focus on. She knew from experience children raised by a single parent, usually the mother, needed that parent to play dual roles, mother and father. She had read publications from eminent people in the field that had arrived at the conclusion children from the nuclear middle-class family, mum and dad, with a bit of money, fared much better in life than children raised by single parents. While she respected the findings she had seen plenty of kids from affluent homes with both parents to care for them run off the rails. On the other hand, she had seen many success stories of people who had grown up in single-parent homes with very little money to spare. Wanting something better was a great driving force. So as far as she was concerned there were two sides to the issue. She was definitely on the side of the single parents and their difficult, challenging role.

She and Julian had a very special relationship in the best and brightest way. She couldn't really say she'd had to work at it. They had loved one another on sight, neither wanting to offer the least little bit of hurt or upset to the other. It might have been a support programme between mother and son. It had worked beautifully.

Other cars were cruising the avenue, looking for a parking spot. A late-model Mercedes shamelessly double parked to take advantage of the fact she might soon be leaving. They were a few metres from the gates of one of the country's top-ranked boys' schools, Kingsley College. The school buildings of dressed stone were regarded by all as exceptionally fine. The grounds were meticulously maintained with great sweeps of emerald green lawn, and a meld of magnificent shade trees. Parents were proud to be able to send their sons there, even if in some cases the fees almost broke the bank.

Thankfully they had found their parking spot when she was really pressed for time. She had received a text message to the effect a meeting with a potential client had been called for first thing in the morning. No name was mentioned.

Briskly Cate bent over to kiss the top of her son's blond head, taking enormous pleasure in the scent of him. His hair was so thick and soft it cushioned her lips. "Love you, darling," she said from the depths of her heart. Ah, the passage of time! She had visions of Jules as the most adorable baby in the world. Jules as a toddler. It seemed only the other day since he had taken his first steps. Wonder of wonders it had been a Sunday and she was at home. She was convinced he had delayed the momentous event so she could witness it; so she could be there for him to half run, half stumble into her waiting arms. Surely it wasn't that long since he had turned four and she had put on a big birthday party with clowns and rides on a darling little Shetland pony in the grounds? It had to be only a few *months* since he had lost his first baby tooth heralding the arrival of the tooth fairy? Time was so precious and Time was passing far too quickly. Her son was being shaped and developed before her eyes. He was rapidly turning into a questioning child, looking at the world from his own perspective.

"Love you too, Mum," Jules answered. It was their daily ritual. The "Jules" had started the very first day of school when his best friend, Noah, had hit on it in preference to the mouthful Julian. Now he was Jules to everyone, his wide circle of friends, classmates, even teachers. He took over-long unfastening his seat belt. He even hesitated a moment before opening out the passenger door.

"Everything okay, sweetheart?" Her mother's antennae picked up on his inaction.

For a moment he didn't answer, as though weighing up the effect his answer might have on her. Jules was super protective. Then it all came out in a rush. "Why can't I have a dad like every-one else?" He spoke in a half mumble, head down, when Jules never mumbled. He was a very clever, confident little boy, much loved and cared for with all the warmth that was vital for the growth of his young body and soul. Jules was no solitary child.

At his words, Cate's heart gave a painful lunge. Deep down, no matter how much he was loved by her, his mother, it seemed Jules longed for a dad; the glory of having a dad, a male figure to iden-tify with. Clearly she couldn't cover both roles. Her mouth went dry.

Haven't you always known you'd have to ad-dress this? The dark cloud over your head, the constant psychological weight.

Adept at masking her emotions, her voice broke halfway. "It's biologically impossible not to have a dad, Jules." A pathetic stopgap, unworthy. Jules was at the age of reason. Everything changed as a child grew to the age of reason. Jules, her baby, was pushing forward. Questions were about to be asked. Answers sought. Her fears would be revealed as secrets became unlocked. This was an area she had to confront.

Now.

"Be serious, Mum," Jules implored. He turned back to her, pinning her with his matchless blue eyes. Everyone commented on the resemblance between them. Except for the eyes. "You don't know what it's like. The kids are starting to ask me all sorts of questions. They never did it before. Who my dad is? Where is he? Why isn't he with us?"

She put it as matter-of-factly as she could. "I told you, Jules. He lives in England. He couldn't be with us."

God, he doesn't even know there's an "us". What would he do if he did? Acknowledge paternity? Easy enough to prove. Let it all go? Not enough room in his life for an illegitimate child? Surely the term illegitimate wasn't used any more? What would he do? Would he act, acknowledge his child? That was the potentially threatening question. Only no one was going to take her son from her. She had reared him. She had shouldered the burden of being a single mother. If it came down to it—a fight for custody—she would fight like a lioness.

Except her case could be unwinnable. No wonder she had woken up that morning feeling jittery. It was as though she was being given a warning.

"Doesn't he love us?" Jules' question snapped her back to attention. "Why didn't he want to be with us? The kids think you're super cool." They did indeed. Jules' mother was right up there in the attention stakes.

Julian's young life had been woman oriented, sublimely peaceful. He lived with his mother, and his grandmother Stella, who had always looked after him, especially when Cate was at work or delayed with endless long meetings. Jules had lots of honorary "aunts"—friends and colleagues of hers. They lived in a rather grand hillside house with a view of the harbour. It was a five-minute drive down to a blue sparkling marina and a park where kids could play. The city, surrounded by beautiful beaches, offered any number of places to go for a swim. Jules was already a strong swimmer for his age. He lived the good life, stable and secure. Jules wanted for nothing.

Except a father.

"Why couldn't you get married, Mum?" Her son's young voice combined protectiveness for her and unmistakable hostility for the man who had fathered him. This was a new development, emotionally and socially. Jules was clearly reviewing his position in his world.

"We were going to, Jules," Cate told him very gently. To think she had actually *believed* it. "We were deeply in love, starting to make plans." Their romance had been close to sublime until they had started making plans. Plans did them in. "And then something rather momentous happened. Your father came into an important inheritance called a peerage. That meant he would never leave England." *Didn't want to leave England.* "I was desperate to come back to Australia. My family was here. His people were there. His *life* was there. It was as simple and disruptive as a grand inheritance. Your father's mother had someone in mind for her only son. She was the daughter of an earl. Born to the purple, as it were." Even now the breath rushed out of her chest.

Your paternal grandmother, with her silk knickers in a twist. Alicia, the patrician-faced hatchet woman who expected Cate to do the right thing and go home.

"Didn't she like you?" Jules sounded incredulous. His mother was perfect in his eyes.

Cate had to acknowledge she still bore the scars of that last confrontation with Alicia, the icy determination of the woman, the breathtaking arrogance of the English upper class. "Well, she did at first," she managed after a moment. It was true enough. Alicia had been supremely confident this young woman was going back to Australia. It was no more than a holiday flirtation, a passing fancy for a pretty girl. But there were strict limits to the friendship. The question of succession had finally been settled. "Later I was made very aware there was no question of a marriage between us."

"None at all, my dear. How could you think otherwise? My son will marry one of us." Alicia had been adamant. Here was a woman with a deep understanding of *noblesse oblige*.

She must have muttered aloud, because Jules asked with a flash to his beautiful eyes, "Who's *us?*"

"Oh, I soon discovered that!" She gave a brief laugh. "People of the same background. The English aristocracy and the like. It's still a class system no matter what they say."

"Class system?" Jules was getting het up.

That wouldn't do. "It's different from here, Jules," she said soothingly. "Don't worry about it. I'll explain it to you this evening."

"So he married someone else, the *us?*" Anger simmered in Jules' clear voice. Another stage in his development.

"I expect so. I never followed through. I left him and England behind, my darling. My life is here, Jules. With you and Nan. You're happy, aren't you?"

Jules rallied. He wasn't going to upset his mother any further. "Sure I'm happy, Mum," he declared, though it was obvious to Cate he was grappling with this fresh information. He leant over to give her a kiss. "I can take care of the boys at school. What's his name, my father's name?"

"Ashton." She suddenly realised she had not spoken his name *aloud* for years. *Ashe. Julian Ashton Carlisle, Fifth Baron Wyndham.*

"That's a funny name," Jules said. "Bit like Julian. I expect he named me. English, you see. I'm glad everyone calls me Jules. Better go, Mum. See you tonight."

"Take care, my darling."

"I will." Jules gave her a quick hug. Mercifully Jules wasn't one of those kids who were embarrassed by public displays of affection. Noah, on the other hand, had forbidden his mother to kiss him when any of the other kids were about. Jules made short work of heaving up his satchel then hopping out of the car. Noah was racing towards him both arms outstretched, one up, one down, dipping and rising mimicking a plane's wings. He was calling out in delight, "Jules…Jules…"

Cate watched a moment longer, her heart torn. *May joy fill your days.* Both boys turned back to wave to her. She responded, putting a big carefree smile on her face.

This is only the start of it all, my girl. Her inner voice broke up the moment, weighing in with a warning.

At twenty-six she was well on the way to becoming a high flyer in the corporate world. She knew she appeared to others to have it all. Only one person, Stella, the person closest to her, knew the whole story. She could never have managed without Stella's selfless support. It was Stella who had taken charge of her baby when she was at university. She needed a career. They had both agreed on that. She had a son to rear.

Stella was the guardian angel for her and her son. Stella, her adoptive mother.

It had taken well over twenty years for her to find out who her biological mother was. And that only came about because her biological mother had thought it prudent to make a deathbed confession before she met her Maker.

A sad way to clean the slate; devastating for an unacknowledged daughter to find out the truth. Sometimes she thought she would never forgive Stella for not having told her. Over the years she had met "Aunty Annabel" perhaps a half dozen times when she visited Stella, her older sister in Australia. Cate realised then, as never before, one should not keep secrets from a child. Inevitably at some stage it would all come out causing confusion and conflict and often estrangement. She'd had her own experience as an adult. She couldn't delay all that much longer discussing her past with her child. What choice did she have? Questions would be repeated over and over if the issue wasn't addressed. She couldn't allow her old emotions to get in the way.

"Good morning, Cate." It was the attractive young brunette behind the reception desk.

"Morning, Lara."

Lara was busy appraising Cate's smart appearance. "Mr Saunders and the others are waiting for you in the boardroom. Some bigwig is coming in."

"Have you got a name for me?" Cate paused to enquire.

"Actually, no." Lara sent her a look of mild surprise. "The appointment is for nine-fifteen. Love your outfit." Lara had learned a great deal about grooming, hair, make-up, clothes accessories, simply from studying Cate Hamilton. Cate had such style. She was wonderfully approachable too. No unbearable airs of superiority, unlike Cate's female colleague, the terrifying Murphy Stiller, who held herself aloof from everyone not on the command chain. Stiller was supremely indifferent to office perceptions of her. Cate Hamilton appeared to know instinctively office alliances were important.

"Thanks, Lara." Cate moved off. In her own spacious office she swiftly divested herself of her classic, quilted lambskin black handbag, and then checked her appearance in the long mirror she'd had fixed inside the door of one of the tall cabi-

nets. She always dressed with great care. It was
important to look good. It was expected of her. It
went with the job. She was wearing a recent buy,
a designer two-piece outfit with a slim black pen-
cil skirt and a white jacket banded in black. Her
long blonde hair—the definitive Leo's mane—she
always wore pulled back into various updated ar-
rangements for work. Looking good was mandatory. All-out glamour wasn't on the agenda. Too
distracting to the clients. Even so she'd been told
she was considered pretty hot stuff.

They were all seated around the boardroom table—
big as any two ping-pong tables shoved together—
when she entered the room.

"Good morning, everyone," she greeted them
pleasantly, and received suave nods that hid a variety
of feelings. Downright lecherous on the part of
Geoff Bartz, their resident environmentalist and
a very unattractive man. The hierarchy was still
men, though not as inflexible as it once had been.
The richest person in Australia was in fact a
woman, the late mining magnate Lang Hancock's
daughter, Gina Rinehart, worth around twenty
billion and counting. All of the men were Italian
suited, Ferragamo shod, the one woman at the
table as impeccably turned out as ever, cream silk
blouse, Armani power suit. No one reached a position near the top of the tree without being excep-

tionally well dressed. Lord knew they were paid enough to buy the best even if they rarely strayed from imported labels. Cate trusted her own instincts, giving Australian designers a go. They were so good she stuck to them.

"Ah, Cate," Hugh Saunders, CEO and chairman of the board of Inter-Austral Resources, oil, minerals, chemicals, properties etc. sat at the head of the table. He was credited with almost single-handedly turning a small sleeping mining company into a multibillion-dollar corporation. On Cate's entry he exhaled an audible sigh of pleasure. A lean, handsome, very stylish man turning sixty, he had personally recruited Cate Hamilton some three years previously. He considered himself her mentor. If he were only ten years younger he privately considered he would have qualified as a whole lot more, sublimely unaware Cate had never entertained such a thought. "Come take a seat. There's one here by me." He gestured towards the empty seat to his right.

Territorial display if there ever was one, Murphy Stiller thought with a tightening of her lips and a knitting of her jet-black brows of one. Murphy Stiller was brilliant, abrasive, ferociously competitive. Murphy's sole aspiration was to move into Hugh Saunders' padded chair while it was still warm. The great pity was he was such a stayer! Before Hamilton had arrived on the scene she had been Queen of the Heap, able to command attention and a seat at the CEO's right hand without saying a word. Then the newcomer she had mentally labelled *upstart* had from the outset started producing results. Corporate politics, balance sheets, marketing plans, impromptu presentations, refinancing. It could have been familiar territory. Hamilton was up for the challenge. A compulsive over-achiever, of course. Murphy knew the type. A multitasker, always up to speed. Saunders seemed mesmerised by her. Certainly he had carefully mapped out her career. But that was what men spent a lot of time thinking about, wasn't it? Sex. Whether they were getting it. Or more often missing out. When Murphy had entered the boardroom she had naturally made for the seat on the CEO's right—she never jockeyed, jockeying was beneath her—only to be forestalled by Saunders' upraised hand smoothly directing her to a seat on his left, as though oblivious to her chagrin. Time to hot up her nightly prayers her young rival would get her comeuppance. Flunk something. Take a fall. Get married. Go into politics. Fall under a bus. Anything.

Murphy forced herself to stop daydreaming. It wasn't going to happen.

All were now seated. All faces were turned to the chairman, who had glanced at his watch to check what time they had. "What we do and say here before our prospective client arrives is extremely important," he announced with great earnestness. "This is a man used to meeting people at the highest level. I believe he even talks to the Prince of Wales on a first-name basis."

Cate pretended to be lost in envy. She had her own understanding of the English upper classes, though the Prince was said to be a genuine egalitarian.

"He's already acquired a small empire in different parts of the world," the CEO was saying. "He's now looking at our mineral wealth. Overseas the news is Australia is being driven by mining and resource. Not surprising their top entrepreneurs want in. We're going to prove extremely helpful." He paused as another project came to mind. "He's also interested in acquiring a property in the Whitsundays. Virgin territory as it were, far away from the usual haunts of jetsetters and the current hot spots, the Caribbean and such. You all know the late George Harrison bought up there. Had a holiday home on our far-flung shores, then a virtual outpost. George knew what he was about. I know we can help our prospective client. Perhaps you, Cate. You're very good at dealing with people. You might even be able to persuade Lady McCready to finally sell Isla Bella. She trusts you. Aren't many places left in the world as pristine as Isla Bella."

"Sure our prospective client doesn't want to turn

it into a resort?" Cate asked. "Lady McCready is totally against any such project."

"Goodness me, no!" Saunders vehemently shook his head as though he'd had it straight from the horse's mouth. "This is a man who shuns glitz. He wants a private sanctuary for him, his family and close friends. He will want to visit, of course, if Lady McCready is agreeable. She must be a great age now. Only the other day someone told me she had passed away."

"Still very much alive, sir," Cate said, watching the CEO hold up a staying hand as the mobile on the table rang. He listened for a moment, said a few words, then put the receiver down. "Ah, he's arrived."

It was delivered with such reverence the prospective client could equally well have been Prince Charles or even President Obama. The Clintons had made the great escape to North Queensland and the Great Barrier Reef islands, pronouncing the whole area an idyllic destination. Perhaps it was Bill Clinton or some retired American senator, who just wanted to sit around all day without anyone taking cheap shots at him as political enemies tended to do.

Lara entered the boardroom cheeks glowing, her mouth curved up in a smile. After her came an extremely handsome man in a hawkish kind of way: aquiline nose—perfect to look down on people—

finely chiselled aristocratic features, thick jet-black hair with a natural wave, extraordinary eyes, the colour of blue flame; immediate impact that would linger for a long time. He stood well over six feet, very elegantly dressed. Not Zenga; Savile Row made to measure. A tailor's dream. Snow-white shirt, striped silk tie no doubt denoting something elitist, tied just so. So sophisticated was his appearance it held them all speechless for a while.

But none more transfixed than Cate.

Time collapsed. How vivid was memory; how powerful was the past!

For a fleeting moment she felt her breathing had stopped. Then as air came back into her lungs she knew such fright she thought she had actually fainted while still remaining conscious. Her whole body was shaking, her mind sliding out of kilter. Thank God she didn't have a glass of mineral water in her trembling hand for everyone would have watched her drop it to the ground where it probably would have shattered.

This is it, she thought. The heavens had shifted. She knew he had taken her in at once.

Lord Julian Ashton Carlisle, Fifth Baron Wyndham.

The father of her child.

She had come to him a virgin, the man who had devastated her life. So this was the way Karma worked? Action, effect, fate. She was trapped in the same room as the man she had never succeeded in erasing from her mind or her heart and hated him for it. He was indelibly fixed there by lost love, sorrow and humiliation. She had tried with every atom of her being to put the past behind her, but the past had had its effect on all of her subsequent relationships. No other man measured up.

Now her brain was signalling warnings.

The Day of Reckoning is at hand.

Over the past years she had almost succeeded in convincing herself Jules was solely *hers*. A virgin birth as it were. She knew now she had lost all touch with reality. Jules at some point in his life was going to want to meet his father. Jules' father might very well want to meet the son he had hitherto known nothing about. The only way she could avert such a thing happening was to keep them far apart. At least until Jules was of an age to undertake his own search for his biological father, who probably by now had children with his aristocratic wife. Impeccable breeding, of course. It was expected, after all. Someone had to inherit the baronetcy, keep up tradition. Social status was something to be cherished.

Cate made a massive effort to calm herself by focusing on how appalling things had been for her. Alicia, steely eyed, tall, rail-thin body vibrating as she told her to go away and not come back. All Alicia had ever been up to then had been no more than a bit on the snobbish side—a woman with a mindset stuck in the early twentieth century, very patronising to a young woman from the colonies, but pleasant enough. Then everything had abruptly changed. It had been crisis time, with Ashe away for a few days in London on family business. It had all been stunningly, shockingly sudden.

"There's simply no place for you here, Catrina." Alicia had spoken with a gleam of triumph in her slate-grey eyes. *"My son has acknowledged that. I am sorry for you, my dear, but you allowed yourself false hopes. You made a terrible mistake, but then you're so very young. So ignorant of the ways of the world. Frankly I did try to warn you. There are unwritten rules to our way of life. We all understand them. You don't. You would never have fitted in. Marina was born for the role. Julian may have thought you special for a time, but now he knows he has to take a step back. Life is all about doing one's duty, assuming one's responsibilities."*

Cate hadn't accepted that blindly. She had fought back claiming all were equal under the sun, her expression so combative any other woman but Alicia might have ducked for cover. She'd told Alicia she needed to hear it all from Ashe himself.

Ashe, please help me.

Only Ashe wasn't there.

"That's the thing, my dear. Julian is in London," Alicia had countered, trying to sound pitying and only succeeding in sounding chilling. *"He's not there on business. I assumed you would guess that. He went away because he couldn't bear to tell you himself. It was far from an easy decision but I helped him see it was the best way. Indeed the only way. You are both far too young. Julian simply didn't realise you were taking him so utterly seriously. Holiday romances tend to fade pretty quickly, my dear. You'll find that out when you get back to Australia. You have your own life. My son has his."*

And so she had vanished. It took her a couple of months more to come to the devastating realisation she was pregnant. *Hello, pregnant?* When they had practised safe sex. She had never trusted safe sex from there on. She was pregnant to a young man, to a family, who didn't want her. Moreover would not be eager to know her child even if it had their blood. She wasn't good enough. It was a grave situation and one of her own making. She had turned to the only mother she had ever known to help her.

Stella.

CHAPTER TWO

England, 2005

CATE HAD BEEN driving for miles through the picture-perfect English countryside, a patchwork of emerald-green fields bordered by woods, lovely towering trees and wondrously neat hedges. Miraculously it had stopped raining. She had only been in England a couple of weeks, and the rain had been falling without end. And, Lord, was it *cold!* The European winter was fast setting in. But for now the sun shone, however briefly, and what lay before her was a pastoral idyll, a symphony of soft misty colours. It made her feel good to be alive. On her own at last. Freedom! Was there anything so good? *Freedom.* She sang it aloud. No one to hear her anyway but the woolly white sheep that dotted the enchanting landscape. It was simply wonderful to be footloose and fancy free.

Her base for her gap year was the great historic city of London, squeezed into a *teeny* flat with

two of her university-going pals. Not that they
noticed the lack of life's little luxuries to which
all of them had long been accustomed. They were
too busy enjoying themselves and exploring the
cultural wonders the great city had to offer. This
was to be a great year for them, their Grand Tour.
Afterwards all three would embark on their chosen careers. Josh came from a long line of medical
doctors, so it was Medicine for Josh. Sarah with
her legal family would read Law. Cate had decided
on the high-flying world of Big Business, maybe
along the track of an MBA from Harvard? So that
had meant an Economics degree. At school her
brilliance at Maths had set her apart. That didn't
bother her. She had been something of an oddity
all her life.

Why wouldn't she have been, given her history? She had been raised not knowing who her
biological parents were. That alone put a girl at a
severe psychological disadvantage. But at least she
had been adopted as a baby by a beautiful young
Englishwoman who to her great sadness couldn't
carry a baby beyond a couple of months without
suffering a miscarriage. She had come by all ac-
counts as a gift from God, albeit a giveaway baby
to the right couple. Stella and Arnold certainly
were. She knew they loved her. She loved them.
They were good people, kindness itself, encour-
aging her in every way. But she had never truly

felt she *belonged*. Forever a step away. Despite all their efforts—and she had been a difficult child she had to admit—she was and remained, in her own mind at least, an *outsider*.

Stella had had no idea when Cate left Australia that her adopted daughter fully intended tracking down the Cotswold manor house where Stella and her sister, Annabel, had grown up. "Lady" Annabel, her ravishing adoptive *aunt*, had only visited her sister in Australia a mere handful of times in the last two decades. A true and loving sister. Annabel had remained in England where she married one Nigel Warren, knighted by the Queen for something or other and a seriously rich man many years her senior. Stella, on the other hand, had married someone her own age. The great mystery was Stella and her new husband had abandoned their gracious lives in England to migrate to the opposite end of the earth: *Australia*. An extraordinary move, one would have thought. They hadn't arrived penniless, however. Quite the reverse, which surely had some significance? With private funds they had settled into a new life on the oldest continent on earth.

Surely though they had to be missing all this? Cate thought. Even the softly falling rain had its own enchantment. Home was Home, wasn't it? This part of the world somewhat to her surprise— used as she was to a brilliant, eternally shining sun and vast open spaces—she found truly beautiful. Comforting. *Oddly* familiar. It was as though she had stepped into a wonderful English landscape painting by Constable. One with which she identified. That mystified her. Such a landscape couldn't be further removed from where she had grown up. There the sun dominated. The rain when it came didn't require one to keep a raincoat forever handy—often it required a boat.

For now she was intent on catching a glimpse of the manor house that had been in Stella's family for many years. Yet Stella had chosen to abandon the country of her birth and what had to be a gracious heritage for the comparative wilderness. Cate had to think it was love. Arnold was as English as Stella. Both, even after twenty years, retained their upper-class English accents. A few of her schoolmates in the early days had dared to call her a "Pom". They hadn't done it twice. At least not to her face. But even she knew her accent was more English than English-Australian. Why wouldn't it be the way she had grown up?

She had arrived in the village now, with no idea her life was poised for dramatic change. She pulled to the side of the street, then switched off the ignition of her little hire car, looking keenly around her. The village was so small but very pretty, dominated by what had to be original Tudor buildings with a handful of speciality shops. Glorious hanging baskets featured a spilling profusion of brightly coloured and scented flowers. She spotted a tea room, a picturesque old pub, The Four Swans, and a post office. There was a central park that had a lovely large pond. Over the green glassy surface glided the said four snow-white graceful swans. Her heart lifted. She stepped out of the car, rounding the bonnet, to enter the post office. Graceful in body and movement, she walked fast with a long confident stride.

A pleasant-faced woman carrying too much weight was behind the counter deep into a romance novel. A bodice ripper by the look of it. The woman glanced up with a welcoming smile as Cate entered. "Lost yourself, love?" She inserted a bookmark to mind her place.

Cate had to laugh. She had an excellent sense of direction. "Not really. I was enjoying this very beautiful part of the world."

"So it is. So it is. I'm the postmistress among other things. Aussie, love?"

Cate's smile widened. "At home more often than not I'm mistaken for a Pom."

The woman nodded sagely. "Not the accent, love." Upper-class English, but not *quite*, Joyce Bailey thought. "Something about your easy manner, the confident stride, the attitude."

"Now that is flattery at its finest." Cate gave a little mock bow.

The postmistress leant heavily on the counter. "I have family in Australia. Been out there a couple of times. Ah, life in the sun! The family, especially the kids, won't come back now. They're fair dinkum Aussies. So how can I help you?'

"Radclyffe Hall," Cate said, moving closer. "Which way is it? I'm keen to take a glimpse."

The postmistress abruptly sobered. "Great white elephant of a house. Lots of tragedy in that family. Sons that served in the army. Lost in all sorts of battles. Crimean, Balkan, First and Second World Wars, the Falklands. Enormous devastation, wars! The present Lord Wyndham who inherited when his older brother was killed doesn't entertain much. Not like the old days. But the whole village has learned the historic gardens and the parklands are being restored. Be quite a challenge, I reckon. A famous landscape gardener has been working there for months. His aim is to bring the estate back to its former glory. Best of luck, we all say. We'll have the tourists back in no time. The hall's rose gardens used to be ever so famous. You won't be able to get in, love. But you can enjoy the view. The manor house—it's built out of our lovely honey-coloured Cotswold stone—stands on the top of the hill. Keep driving north out of town, no more than three miles on. Can't miss it. All of them rolling acres belong to Lord Wyndham. Only had daughters. No surviving son. The estate is entailed so it will pass to another male member of the Radclyffe family once Lord Wyndham is gone."

Cate absorbed all this information in utter silence. In truth she was poleaxed. Stella had rarely spoken of her former life. Stella had made secrecy an art form. Cate hadn't even known the house where Stella and her younger sister, Annabel, had grown up was called Radclyffe Hall until fairly recently when she had overheard a conversation between Stella and Arnold. So this all came as a revelation. Lord Wyndham was Stella's father. My God! Wasn't Stella a woman for burying the past? Cate felt incensed but shook it off.

"What's lunch like at the pub?" she asked, swiftly changing the subject. It would take time to absorb it all. Lots of time. Quietness to reflect.

"Second to none!" the postmistress declared stoutly.

"Think they can put me up for a few days?"

"I'd say so, love. Me and my hubby, Jack, run it. Shall I book you in?"

"If you would. My name is Cate Hamilton, by the way. I have ID in the car." She half turned to go out and get it.

"Won't be necessary, love," the woman stayed her. "We'll get the particulars when you return from your sightseeing jaunt. I'll have your room prepared."

"Thank you. You're very kind, Mrs—"

"Bailey. Joyce Bailey."

"Pleasure to meet you, Mrs Bailey." Cate put out her hand. It was heart-lifting to be so warmly received.

Joyce Bailey took it. She just loved that radiant smile. Funny thing was the girl—she couldn't have been more than eighteen—reminded her of someone. She tried to think who. No one who lived in the village. She was absolutely sure of that. She knew every last soul. But the smile, the girl's beauty, struck some sort of chord. Maybe it would come to her some time. Never an oil painting, she suddenly remembered the beautiful Radclyffe girls, Stella and Annabel. Dark-haired both, with lovely melting dark eyes; Annabel had been considered the more beautiful of the two. The whole district had been stunned when Stella and her husband had taken off for Australia. Annabel had gone with them at the time. But Annabel had returned almost a year later to marry a baronet who carried her off to London.

It had taken little time for Lord and Lady Wyndham to adapt to losing their beautiful daughters. The loss of their son, the heir, in infancy was the big tragedy. Everything else rated far below the line. The death of the son had come as the great blow of their lives. Other losses could be sustained. It was well known in the village the Radclyffes were a dysfunctional family.

After Lady Wyndham died, her husband retreated from the world, seeing few visitors. The Australian girl had no chance of getting a glimpse inside the hall. She could get as far as the garden. Beautiful girls had a way of getting in where the ants couldn't.

So her objective Radclyffe Hall was only a few miles away. Cate couldn't help feeling a quickening excitement. She slipped back behind the wheel with a parting wave to Mrs Bailey who, intrigued, had come to the post office door to see her off. Cate was really looking forward to this excursion. Lunch too for that matter. She was hungry. Back on the road there was a continuation of the chequered green landscape, a tapestry with all its different textures. It had the most potent charm. She had the window wound down so she could feel the breeze against her cheek. This was a muted world of soft pastel shades, and a totally different quality of light. Even the underlying colour schemes were different. She was used to such a flamboyant palette.

Just when she thought it was all plain sailing, the engine of the little hire car gave a cough, then a splutter. She urged it onto the verge where it quietly died.

"Blast!" Cate hit the wheel with both hands. Clever she might be at maths, but a car mechanic she was not. She looked ahead, then back. Nothing coming. She could lock the car, then proceed on foot. She couldn't be that far off her objective. But what about getting back again? She got out of the car, setting about lifting the bonnet to have a peer inside. Perhaps the car had overheated and she could restart it after a while. She heard a vehicle coming along the country road behind her. She didn't turn around, trusting whoever it was would stop. Help out a young lady in distress. The English were mannerly helpful people. Or so she'd been told.

The resonant male voice when it came wasn't in the least solicitous. It was unmistakably a young man's voice, but it proclaimed the legendary public-school accent—Eton? Harrow? Maybe modernised a bit.

"Think you can handle it?"

She found herself bridling at the tone. It was shocking in its languidness. "Clear off," she muttered, risking she would be overheard.

He pounced. "I did ask a question."

"Really!" She spun around, shocked by the level of aggression that tone had provoked. "And I'm asking *you* one. What's so funny? Do you want to help or are you just being bloody-minded?" Of course he was. She could spot it.

He gave her an extraordinarily beautiful if condescending smile. Humour the girl. Beautiful white teeth, perfectly even and straight. She felt all her nerve ends clench. "Exaggerating, aren't you?" he asked ever so slowly, at the same time taking her in. "I only enquired if you can handle the problem."

She couldn't mask the irritation his persona engendered. Such feelings had never attacked her before. He was as handsome as the devil. Those *eyes*! She had never seen eyes so intensely blue. Sapphires set in coal-black lashes. A wave of jet-black hair flopped down onto his high forehead. His skin faintly dewed with perspiration was very fine, lightly tanned. He had a nose disagreeable to her. An aquiline *beak*, the bone as straight as a blade. You could get impaled on it. He was using it to good effect looking down it at her. Some girls would really fancy him. Most would actually. "I've never met with a problem up until today," she told him shortly. "A less than efficient hire car, in fact a bit of a rattle trap. Steering a bit wobbly. But it's been okay up to date, which doesn't explain why the engine suddenly died on me."

"Would you allow me to take a look?" he asked, mock super suave. He wafted an elegant hand in the air. The Scarlet Pimpernel dressed like a gardener, square shoulders, narrow hips, tight jeans, navy jersey, a red kerchief tied loosely around his neck for a bit of dash, high muddy boots.

Cate didn't rush to answer. "Know about cars, do you? I didn't catch your name?"

"Nosey Parker," he said, moving to stand beside her. Suddenly she was dwarfed when she wasn't all that short: five-four.

She knew she was being terribly ungracious, but her feelings of hostility were expanding by the minute. "Suits you," she commented.

From peering into the car, he stood to attention running his vivid blue eyes over her flushed face. Eyes that sparkled and snaffled her up. She preferred soft eyes. Gentle, humorous eyes. Brown maybe. "Have you been drinking?" he asked.

She couldn't ignore that. "Right! You can smell the fumes, can you?"

"You could have stopped off at The Four Swans," he answered, continuing to study her keenly.

She might have stepped out of a wrecked space shuttle instead of a beat-up piece of British engineering. Cate's blonde head snapped up. "Ha, ha and ha! Apart from being nosey, you're downright rude."

"No different from you," he returned with the arrogance that had to be bred into him. "Looks like we've rubbed each other up the wrong way."

"You don't stand a chance of rubbing up against me," she said tartly. "So what's wrong with the car, or don't you know? I'd say you were used to leaving all that to the chauffeur. No doubt you're the centre of someone's solar system?"

"Perfectly true. How did you know?" He got into the car, making a business of squirming before cranking back the seat as though the car had previously been driven by a midget. He then switched on the engine, which kicked over briefly, then gave up the ghost. "The reason for your breakdown— tempestuous little Aussie that you are—is you're out of petrol," he announced as he got out.

For a moment Cate was seriously embarrassed. "Nonsense! It was reading a quarter full. Or near enough. And stop staring at me as though I'm from another planet."

He laughed. "To be perfectly honest I didn't know extraterrestrials came ravishingly pretty."

Had she blushed? Damn it, she had. "Don't feel the need to flatter me."

"I thought it was a plain statement of fact. As for my opinion of your manner? Prickly as a rose bush. Now, the petrol gauge is obviously not reading true. Where are you going anyway?"

She backtracked. "How did you know I'm an Australian?" she asked as though that created a definite barrier.

"I'd rather not say." He shut his mouth firmly. It was a very good mouth, a clean sensual line above his chiselled jaw. The edges were faintly upturned. She found herself noting all the little details. She really had to concentrate on something other than his mouth. She felt in her bones he would be a great kisser. It would be interesting to see what happened if he suddenly grabbed her.

"Why would that be?"

"Maybe I'm frightened you'll attack me." His sapphire eyes were alive with mockery.

Did her heart turn over? Something in her chest did. Even her legs were feeling a bit flimsy. Nevertheless she took a step forward. "You find Australians threatening?"

Instantly he took a step back, holding up his elegant hands in a gesture of appeasement. "On the contrary, I like Australians. Within reason."

Cate gave up. He had a very engaging laugh. It made her want to laugh back. "I was on my way to Radclyffe Hall. You would know it."

"Why exactly?" he asked, with an unexpected frown. "Why Radclyffe Hall?"

Cate's turn to frown. "Look, can't we drop the interrogation? I just want to look at it."

"Then you'll have to do it from afar," he said.

"I never said I wanted to drop in for tea and scones." She tilted her chin. God, he was tall! "What's your name, by the way?"

"Ashe."

"Ash?" She raised a supercilious brow. "Your parents called you Ash?" she asked, feigning incredulity. "I've never met anyone called Ash. I take it that's Ashe with an e?"

"Julian Ashton," he informed her, looking impossibly, unbearably superior. "And you are?"

She considered not telling him. Only she could use his help. "Catrina Hamilton. My family and friends call me Cate."

"Then I shall call you Catrina."

"That's okay. Please do, *Ashe*. So are you going to help me out?"

He shrugged a shoulder. His body was perfectly proportioned, giving the strong impression of superb physical fitness. "How can I? I'm heading in the opposite direction," he retorted carelessly.

Cate didn't know what to make of that. "I understood Englishmen were gentlemen," she said with sudden dismay. "You must be a rare species."

He shook his head, loosening the satiny black wave that had stuck to his forehead. "Our womenfolk are much sweeter and more persuasive than you." He sounded deeply grateful for the fact.

"You must know only quiet, controllable creatures. Does this mean you're going to leave me stranded on a lonely country road?"

He considered a while, looking this way and that. "An apology might be in order," he suggested.

"We take it in turns, do we?" she asked. Goodness, he could only be a handful of years older than she, maybe twenty-three or four, but with an imperiousness well beyond his years.

"Okay then. I'm off." From nonchalance he was energised, turning purposefully towards his parked four-wheel drive.

"So much for being a gentleman, then," she called after him severely. "Go on. Drive away." He looked very much as if he was going to. "All right, *sorry.*" She only said it because that was what he wanted.

Immediately he swung back, beckoning her towards his vehicle, a dusty banged-up Range Rover. "Come along," he called briskly as though it were possible he'd change his mind. "I'll run you up to the hall, then send someone back with a can of petrol to pick up your old bomb. The only thing that surprises me is you didn't finish up in a ditch."

Cate swallowed a put-down. No need to antagonise him further. Maybe his turning up was an omen?

Good or bad she couldn't yet tell.

Courteously he held the door for her. His fingers brushed against hers, setting off such an explosion of sparks it almost had her crying, "Ouch!"

Inside the battered Range Rover, the sparks continued to jump the distance between them. It radiated a heat through her body, to her arm, her breasts, her stomach, working its way lower. Every last nerve ending seemed to be on fire. What she had to do was separate her body from her mind. *Difficult.* She was experiencing the sort of dizziness one had when in the company of someone overwhelmingly attractive. He was definitely *not* gay. She had gay mates. Love was love wherever cupid's arrow fell was her reasoning. This guy was powerfully heterosexual. Married? She found herself hoping he wasn't. He was too young for a start.

He stopped the Range Rover at a certain point. She could see why. It offered a sublime view of Radclyffe Hall. It sat high on a hill overlooking the beautiful countryside and the rolling hills.

It was an extraordinary moment for Cate. She felt a disconcerting prick of tears, blinking them back before he saw them. Whatever she had been expecting, the postmistress's "great white elephant of a house" in an advanced state of decay, it surely wasn't this. She couldn't remain in the vehicle. She threw open the door and jumped out onto the lush green verge, holding a hand to her sunstruck eyes.

He joined her, staring down at her as though faintly perplexed. "Not what you expected?"

Her tone was soft, almost reverent. "Wow, oh, wow! To be honest I'm a bit in shock."

"Why exactly?" He sounded as though he really wanted to know.

She almost told him why. It was on the tip of

her tongue. The moment when she would confide her adoptive mother was Stella Radclyffe that was. Only caution, grounded in childhood, took over. She didn't know it then but her secret history was in the making.

"Well, it's some house, so *grand*. Georgian, I think. The symmetry, the balance, the adherence to classical rules. Chimneys rising to either side of the gabled roof." One-storey wings had been built to the left and right of the imposing central building most probably at a much later date.

"Correct," he said briefly, his eyes glittering. "The hall was built in the late fifteen hundreds by Thomas Willoughby-Radclyffe of Cotswold stone. It's stood for over four hundred years but for a long time now it's been in great need of repair. The house and the estate—it's been reduced to around three hundred acres with tenant cottages—belong to Lord Wyndham. He hasn't enjoyed good health for some time now. In fact he's quite frail."

Four hundred years?

Shock wasn't too strong a word. Why had it been so important to Stella to cover up her past? "Do you know Lord Wyndham?" she turned to ask, her eyes on his profile. Oddly enough she was getting used to that aquiline beak.

"I'm working on a large project there at the moment," he said by way of a response. An eva-

sion if ever there was one. "The restoration of
the hall's once famous gardens, particularly the
rose gardens. It had become something of a wilderness, quite a challenge, but Lord Wyndham
hired a world-famous landscape designer, David
Courtland."

She was fortunate she had grown up with a passionate gardening team, Stella and Arnold, who
had passed on their passion to her. "I've heard of
him." She nodded. "I'm assuming you're the gardener?"

"You could say that."

"A pretty posh one, if you don't mind my saying
so." Her amazing lime-green eyes flashed mockery.

"Don't mind in the least. If you're very good
between here and the hall I'll let you see over the
garden. It has a number of 'rooms' but Dave has
begun a new project. He's in London for a couple
of days."

"Leaving you in charge? Call him Dave, do
you?" she asked provocatively.

"The first strike against you," he clipped off.

"Ah, come on."

"Get back in the car."

"Certainly, m'lord."

And so it began. The great star-crossed love af-
fair of her life.

CHAPTER THREE

The present.

HUGH SAUNDERS stood up to perform the introductions, a delighted smile on his lean, tanned face. Each member of the team and their specific function was acknowledged. Handshakes all round. Murphy Stiller's habitual glare was replaced by a sunburst. When it came to Cate's turn she actually considered fleeing the room, like a woman teetering on the brink of a major crack-up. For all the little niggles of nameless anxiety the last thing her mind had focused on was this momentous blast from the past. Would he now confound her and say, "But I know you, surely? It's Catrina Hamilton, isn't it?" all the while pinning her with his blazing blue eyes?

He did no such thing. Not a muscle on his striking face moved. He calmly took her hand. God, was she bound to him for ever? Even that brief, cool contact evoked such grief, such remembered pain she almost moaned. This time it seemed he had no mind to be cruel. All that came was the usual rhetorical "how do you do?" requiring no answer. Somehow she was able to resume her seat. She had to cast out her devils. And fast. At least her blood was coursing around her body again. A few fraught moments, then she was able to regain enough composure to not put her job in jeopardy.

As CEO, Hugh Saunders dealt with matters mostly but when he turned for her input she was able to contribute from a wealth of research. Her brain was on autopilot. Not for the first time in her career but never when she was in such a high emotional state.

"Absolutely right, Cate." Hugh spoke with approval. Always rely on Cate to give clear concise answers, he thought. Nothing routine. Outside the box. She was one classy young woman, with high-grade diplomacy skills. He admired her capacities and shrewd gut instincts. Gut instincts he considered important. They provided an edge. Even more importantly, never once in his experience had she attempted to capitalise on her beauty.

For some reason Murphy Stiller had suffered a collapse of her usual supreme confidence so Cate was invited to speak out more often. It might have been a triumph despite Murphy's periodic grunts. Murphy was looking a bit as if she wanted to kill someone, preferably Cate. Cate for her part was falling back heavily on experience. Wyndham's questions when they came were brusque, very explicit. It was obvious to everyone seated around the table he was well acquainted with big business, Money Business. They all knew it was conducted in a certain way, bland enough on the surface, underneath extremely tough. He wasn't relying on his advisors. He was managing his own negotiations. While the team was taking the fifth Baron Wyndham's measure he was taking theirs. In the course of the meeting it was revealed he had substantial investments in the mining sector of Chile and Canada. Although the vast State of Western Australia was the usual target for their investors, Cate suggested Queensland as an excellent alternative. Mining drove the Queensland economy just as it did W.A. The traditional bases of wealth created over several generations were being overtaken by mining magnates, some of them surprisingly young. These men were fast rising to the top of the Rich List, rubbing shoulders with the multibillionaires.

Eventually the meeting broke up. Discussions had been intense. A follow-up meeting was scheduled for midweek.

Cate was still concerned he was going to expose her. As what, for God's sake? No one on the planet outside Stella knew Lord Wyndham was the father of her child. Not a single soul since dear Arnold had passed away after two very painful years of battling lung cancer. Her adoptive father always had smoked too much.

Hugh's up mood was infectious. They were moving out of the boardroom, when he suddenly brought up Wyndham's other interest. Buying land on some beautiful Whitsunday island.

"Just a moment, Cate." For some reason Cate was moving away too fast.

"Yes, sir." She turned back.

"Cate here might very well have the answer to your Barrier Reef island retreat," he told Wyndham.

"No." Wyndham responded suavely.

"Cate works hard at everything she does," said Hugh. "She has managed to build a very good relationship with a lady, Lady McCready actually, now in her mid-eighties, who owns a small but fabulous Whitsunday island called Isla Bella."

"After one of Italy's great gardens perhaps or simply a beautiful island?" he asked without looking at Cate.

"Lady McCready did confide she and her husband named their island after a trip to Italy," Cate said. "They loved Italy and the wonderful gardens."

Now he looked down his blade of a nose at her. "The island is for sale?"

"Could be. Could be," Hugh broke in, somewhat puzzled by a certain tension in the atmosphere. He had an instinct for such things.

"You have doubts, Ms Hamilton?" Wyndham asked, his tone faintly brittle.

"Up to a point, yes. Lady McCready is very much against exploitation of her island. No boutique hotels for the rich and their…friends. Certainly no tourist destination. The island has been her home since the death of her husband. She would never be budged on an investment."

Before Hugh could intervene Wyndham pre-empted him. "Let me make it quite clear, Ms Hamilton. It's a private home I wish to build. A tropical retreat for me and my family. Hopefully a few friends will be allowed. I'm a very busy man. Occasionally I like getting away from it all. This is the first trip I've been able to make to Australia. I very much like what I see. The Great Barrier Reef is one of the great wonders of the world. I intend to see it while I'm here."

"Wonderful!" Hugh said, giving Cate the beginnings of a sharpish look. "If you are seriously interested, perhaps Cate could contact Lady McCready. She trusts Cate, you see."

For a fleeting instant Wyndham looked as though he wouldn't trust her for a minute. "Perhaps we could discuss it over dinner this evening," he suggested, as though formalising the matter, making it a business call.

"Cate?" Hugh prompted, his grey gaze turning faintly steely.

Hugh was as near to perturbed as she had seen him. Her behaviour, she knew, wasn't being consistent. She always did what was expected. The intelligent, indeed the only, thing to do.

Her training took over. "Certainly, Lord Wyndham," she said, demonstrating her loyalty to the firm. "That would be lovely. I could in the meantime see if I can contact Lady McCready."

"With that happy thought in mind," he said smoothly, "perhaps you can recommend a restaurant. You know Sydney. I don't."

"C'est Bon!" Cate and Hugh said together.

"I could pick you up at your hotel," Cate said, trying hard to be charming for Hugh's sake. "Shall we say eight o'clock?"

"Are you sure I couldn't pick you up at your home?" Wyndham asked, a glitter in his sapphire eyes. "A limo has been put at my disposal."

"It's quite a drive," said Cate quite untruthfully. "Really, Lord Wyndham, it suits me perfectly to pick you up. No trouble at all."

"Well, that's settled!" Hugh made the emphatic announcement while wondering at the same time what was going on. The fact Cate and Lord Wyndham were antagonistic hadn't been lost on him. I wasn't as though Wyndham didn't approve of career women. He had caught the gleam of respect in his razor-sharp glance as Cate demonstrated her expertise. Perhaps they would settle down over dinner. He sincerely hoped so. This was a big deal for Inter-Austral. Wyndham was prepared to invest a heap of money. Obviously the man was massively rich. Cate was right: Queensland was emerging as *the* hot spot. The state had huge potential expanding on the back of the resources sector. Australia for that matter had one of the highest concentrations of wealth in the world: one super-rich individual per eight thousand or so as opposed to around thirty-seven thousand globally. Lord Wyndham had come to the right place.

Stella, an exceedingly observant woman, saw the upset in Cate's face the moment she walked through the door. It was as still as a marble carving. "Cate, what's up? Are you going to tell me?" Stella, whose whole background had been a gigantic puzzle, perversely demanded she know everything in Cate's life. It had taken Cate many long years to realise Stella in her own quiet way was very controlling.

Cate put her expensive leather handbag down on the marble-topped console in the entrance hall, wondering how best to break the momentous news.

Stella took her silence for refusal and began to walk away, obviously offended.

Cate followed Stella, taking hold of her arm. "Where's Jules?" she asked urgently.

Stella turned to stare at her. "Why, he's in his bedroom playing the video game you bought him. He's done his homework. Never have to tell him. He really is a remarkable child."

"Come into the living room." Cate kept her voice significantly lower. It was their favourite room, furnished with a mix of Asian and Western antiques. Three plush white leather sofas faced the magnificent view across the sparkling blue satin water to the Harbour Bridge and the Opera House. The wide covered deck to the rear was the only major structural change they had made. It had been worth every penny.

"So what is it, then?" Stella set a silk cushion aside as she continued to study the face of her adopted daughter. Both of them had kept Annabel's secret and agreed they would continue to. Cate, however, had stopped calling Stella Mum. Whether she was aware of it or not she had never really thought of Stella as her mum. Jules called Stella Nan. Maybe it wasn't going to stay that way, Cate thought with a funny little stab of premonition.

"Something extraordinary happened today," she

announced, collapsing beside Stella. "I have trouble even getting it out."

"You might try," Stella said, a formless anxiety starting to spread through her. "You've lost your job?" She squeezed her eyes shut. Cate lived such a high-powered life. She handled incredible sums of money. Could something have gone wrong? Big mistakes happened.

"That might have been easier." Cate impatiently kicked off her high-heeled shoes. "I can't put off telling you—"

"But you *are*, dear," Stella stressed somewhat impatiently.

Cate had seen that coming. "All right! You have to know. Of all the men in the world—you're not going to believe this, so steel yourself—Julian Carlisle, the present Baron Wyndham, walked into the boardroom this very morning."

Stella threw up her arms as though she were going to dive into water. "For God's sake!" Now she bent over as if in pain, winding her arms tight around her body like some form of shield.

"Exactly," Cate seconded grimly. Since the revelation that Annabel was her mother, not Stella, Stella's penchant for secrecy loomed large in Cate's mind.

"Has he come in search of you?" Stella asked, as though sensing big trouble ahead. "Has he come in search of Jules?"

"How could he? He knows nothing about Jules." Cate was sorry for the way the colour had faded out of Stella's face. In her early fifties, Stella was still a fine-looking woman. She had kept her slim figure; her thick dark hair was stylishly cut. She had excellent skin and lovely dark eyes. There was no physical resemblance between aunt and niece. For that matter, Cate didn't even resemble her biological mother, Annabel. Annabel never had confessed who Cate's father was, but he had to have been blond with light eyes. "He doesn't know Jules exists," Cate said so harshly, she might have been willing it to remain so. "I'm certain he hasn't found out anything in all these years. He had his own life then. He has it now. I've been no part of it. Probably a vaguely unpleasant memory."

"You hardly came from the wrong side of the tracks," Stella burst out indignantly. "I never did understand why you didn't tell him about us."

"My God, Stella, that's good coming from you." Cate couldn't help ramming that point home. "How would I have known about *us* when you told me nothing? It was as if it was none of my business."

Stella flushed. The truth was hard to take. "I was trying to protect you."

"Protecting your little sister was your main priority," Cate responded bluntly.

"I loved her." Stella spoke as though Cate was

lacking in sensitivity for not understanding. "I looked after her all my life. My mother certainly wasn't interested in us. Neither was my father." Stella's calm face was suddenly bitter. "They mourned the loss of our brother instead." Stella's mind was racing ahead, envisaging a monumental disturbance to her world. "Is Wyndham a potential client?" she asked with faint hope.

Cate nodded, sure a reckoning was in the air. "Apparently he's got truckloads of money. He wants to invest in our mineral resources. Hugh was over the moon."

"I bet," Stella said acidly, struggling to take it all in. "He recognised you, of course." In maturity Cate was even more beautiful than she had been as a ravishingly pretty teenager.

"Of course." Cate reached out to pat Stella's hand. "You know how Hugh likes to put me forward?"

"I've told you before, Cate, the man is in love with you," Stella said with distinct disapproval. Why, Hugh Saunders was even older than she was.

Cate pulled a wry face. "Be that as it may, I have no such interest in Hugh. I'm sure he's got the message."

"They never get the message," said Stella flatly. "Anyway, go on."

"Apparently Lord Wyndham, that relative of yours—"

"And *yours*—" Stella drew her attention to the fact.

"I refuse to acknowledge that," said Cate. "Anyway, he wants to buy or build a tropical hideaway in North Queensland, specifically the Whitsundays. Hugh immediately seized on Lady McCready's retreat, Isla Bella."

"But surely she doesn't want to sell?" Stella asked. "I remember you told me how adamant she was when Keith Munro, the developer, wanted to buy it. She's probably deeded it to a relative. She's a good age."

"Eighty-five. I spoke to her this afternoon." Cate's voice, another of her assets, turned low and ironic. "She's prepared to meet Lord Wyndham."

"Oh, capital!" Stella cried, throwing up her hands. "The *Lord* Wyndham did it, I suppose?"

"Sure helped. After all, your father was the fourth Baron Wyndham, was he not? One would have thought he was a criminal, you kept it so quiet. The thing is Lady McCready doesn't have the right sort of relative to leave Isla Bella to. She believes any one of them would sell it on the spot. So I guess the right buyer thinking of a private retreat might appeal. I'm sure he means what he says. Bring the wife and kids, and some close friends."

"He married her, then?" Both Cate and Stella had fully expected it. "What was her name again?'

"Marina," Cate supplied briefly. She had never

felt any bitterness towards Marina. Marina wasn't to blame for anything. Her bitterness was reserved for Ashe and his dreadful snob of a mother who had given Lady Marina the thumbs up.

"So you're expected to arrange a deal?" Stella asked. Hugh Saunders had told her once Cate was going to go to "the very top"!

"That's what Hugh wants," Cate replied. "It would mean a trip to the island. It would mean a day or so in the company of the man who betrayed me."

"See you don't let it happen twice," Stella warned, sharply. "I'd go mental if you did. You've never got over him."

It was a flat-out accusation. "Maybe not," Cate said, wincing at the harshness of Stella's attack, "but I'm over the torment. I'm my own woman. And I have you and my beautiful boy. He mustn't see Jules." Cate heard the fear in her own voice.

"All you have to do is keep calm," Stella urged, though she too had gone white.

"Not that Jules resembles him—"

"Except for the eyes," Stella was swift to point out. "I went to school with a relative of his, Penelope Stewart, as I'm sure I've told you."

"God, that's a breakthrough!" Cate only half joked. "I'm equally sure you haven't. I would have remembered. I have a photographic memory, you might recall. You've always carried your past in your *head*, Stella. Locked it up and threw away the key."

"I'm sure I told you." Stella decided to hold firm, when she knew perfectly well she hadn't. Her past life was deeply private, even from Cate. Let the secret life be the secret life was her motto. "Penelope's brother, Rafe, was another one madly in love with Annabel." She dropped an involuntary snippet, her tone suggesting that was a very bad thing.

"Really?" Cate was taken aback. "Another thing you've never mentioned before. Tell me, Stella, is this a kind of paranoia you have, this difficulty with speaking about the past?"

"Maybe it is." Stella wasn't about to talk it over. "But the past is past. It's no longer important." She shrugged off what could well have been of grave importance.

"Now that's where you've got it all wrong," Cate murmured sadly. "The past is never past. It follows us around like our shadow. We can't hit the delete button and *whoosh* it's gone."

"May I contradict you there?" Stella said with an odd expression.

"I was expecting you to. But my view is, we're never free of the past, Stella. Especially when much of it is desperate to get through."

Stella gave an ironic smile. "You're referring to Annabel."

Cate nodded. "Annabel, my mother. She certainly got around." Cate sounded both sad and deeply disillusioned. "One wonders who my father was...*is*? He could still be alive and well."

Stella said nothing. She was a little tired of Cate's truth seeking. She pressed her two hands together. Jules' beautiful blue eyes always came as a jolt. So did Cate's golden colouring and green eyes. The past was where so many bad things happened. No wonder she had shut it down.

Cate shook off a prickling sensation at her nape. She continued to stare at her aunt. Of the two of them Stella appeared to be more devastated by the news Julian Carlisle was in town, almost on their doorstep as it were. How come? "*Could* it have been this Rafe?" she abruptly asked, feeling an element of shock.

Stella bit hard on her bottom lip, then surprisingly gave a sour laugh. "I have no idea, Cate. Truly. Annabel never breathed a word. I asked her and asked her. All she ever said was, *Please don't, Stell.* After a while I gave up. She never told me even on the day she died."

Many things were starting to occur to Cate. Unanswered questions asserting themselves strongly. "Maybe she didn't *know*?" Her laugh had a tremor in it.

"She never wanted to hurt you, Catrina," Stella

said, as though Cate really should get her act together.

"But she hurt *you*. She must have been incredibly selfish, self-centred. She fooled you, about a lot of things. She not only fooled you she practically forced you and Arnold to emigrate. You gave up the life you had known. You sacrificed yourself for your promiscuous little sister."

Stella appeared in no rush to refute it. "It was no great sacrifice," she said. The only trouble was it came out unexpectedly virtuous. "I never thought my parents would say, *Please don't go, Stella,* though they gave me a huge wedding. Expected, you know. But look, Cate, you more than made up for it. Arnold and I took you to our hearts on sight. I was never able to bear a child. I don't think it was my fault, rather poor old Arnold's. But we were happy."

"Were you?" Cate flicked her aunt a sceptical glance.

"Well, not *exactly* happy, but good enough. We left our burdens behind. We loved this country, the freedom and the climate. Most of all we had *you*. Have you any idea what a joy that was? You are my own blood, Cate."

"Well, you jolly well could have told me," Cate said, thinking the hurt would never go away.

Stella had long since formed the habit of shrugging off her sins of omission. "So you're always going to blame me?" she asked, as though questioning Cate's capacity for forgiveness.

Cate shook her head when she wasn't at all sure. "I love you, Stell. Let's not talk blame. Things happen in life. But for now, we both know it's not safe for Wyndham to catch sight of Jules."

"God, no!" Stella shuddered.

"It's possible he'll spot a resemblance."

"Bound to," Stella said, as if that would be the horror of horrors. "Are you thinking what I'm thinking? He could acknowledge him?" Stella's slim body tensed up at the thought. She loved Jules. He could have been her own grandchild.

"How do I know?" Cate exclaimed. "Times have changed. Fathers, even of high social standing, are acknowledging children they never knew they had all the time," she said sharply. "For all I know he might have a couple of daughters. We now know the firstborn to British royalty male or female can inherit the throne. Which I think is as it should be. I don't know about entailed inheritances that always went to the male. There's even a possibility Wyndham and his Marina split up. I could've found out if I'd wanted to."

"But you've never wanted to," Stella said. "And I had my own grief, of course." Grief she had openly expressed. "Only Annabel attended my father's funeral. I was told to keep away. *Don't come. Please don't come, Stell. It's not as though*

he will know, but questions will be asked. She
pleaded and pleaded with me, my self-centred little sister. She was absolutely terrified. As usual I
gave in, coming once more to Annabel's rescue. It
wasn't as though I didn't have more pressing concerns. You'd returned home from England sunk
in despair, however hard you'd sought to hide it. It
hadn't taken all that much longer to be faced with
the reason. You were pregnant. Then of course it
all came out."

*Julian bloody Carlisle! The Radclyffes, the Car-
lisles and Others.*

Cate's voice snapped Stella back to the present.

"I had to turn my back on what had happened
to me," Cate was saying. "It was the only way to
survive."

Stella's reaction was on the instant. "You had
me. There's no reason for Carlisle to come near
the house?"

"This is going to further amaze you." Cate gave
a hollow laugh. "We're having dinner tonight."

Stella tapped her forehead so hard she could
have cracked it open. *"Wh-a-a-t?"* Nothing would
ever be the same again. She was sure of it. "Is it
the anniversary of your split?" she asked, a real
bite in her voice. She was terribly perturbed about
Julian Carlisle's re-entry into Cate's life. Cate had
had to work super hard to take up her life. They
had built a life together. They had Jules. They

didn't need anyone else. It would be terrible if Cate thought differently. Cate was, after all, a beautiful young woman living without a man. Cate could rebel. That fact wasn't lost on Stella.

Cate rose to her feet, her golden hair and her luminous skin drawing in all the light. "I'm okay, Stella," she said, bending down to kiss Stella's cheek. "Don't worry. Hugh more or less forced this one on me. He doesn't want to lose Wyndham. Dinner is in the nature of a business call. He wanted to pick me up but I assured him it would be easier for me to pick him up at his hotel. I don't want him anywhere near the house."

"Dear, oh, dear!" Stella looked at her in extreme agitation. Her hands were starting to shake. "Hang on a second, would Hugh Saunders have mentioned at any stage you have a son?"

"I don't think he'd want to get tangled up with all that," Cate said, with a sudden frown. "I have to go, Stell. I need to see Jules, then I have to shower and dress."

"Wait, wait, wait," Stella implored, jumping up. "Someone is bound to tell him. That dreadful Murphy Stiller perhaps? You're a single mother and all that." She knew Cate withheld a great deal of information about herself. A well established family trait.

Cate's green eyes were glittering like gems. "If

need be I can come up with a convincing story. Anyway, it's none of his business."

"That's where you're wrong, Cate," Stella said, her fine features drawn tight. "You'll see if he ever finds out."

It was a possibility neither of them could afford to ignore.

In the end she chose a dinner staple, the little black dress she felt confident in. She enlivened it with the right jewellery. She wasn't out to make any statement. This wasn't a dinner date. This was business, albeit agonising. He had always loved her hair long and loose so she pulled the mass of it back from her face, arranging it in a modern update of the classic chignon. Her only concession was her satin heels. She had to have her heels. Anyway, he was so tall. Gave him a natural advantage.

"You look beautiful, Mummy," Jules pronounced when she went downstairs for inspection. "How come this man isn't picking *you* up?" His mother's male friends always picked her up at the house, not the other way around.

"Easier this way, darling." She put her hand on his squared little shoulder. No sloping there. "Bedtime nine o'clock. What are you going to do?"

"Watch a video with Nan. *Happy Feet*." Jules looked up at Stella. They were great friends. "This man, he's a lord?" Jules asked with interest. "I bet he's a big snob?"

"Only on his mother's and father's side," Cate replied, ruffling his thick hair.

Both Jules and Stella laughed.

"I'll walk you to the car," Jules said, taking Cate's hand. Cate had left the BMW out on the driveway lined on one side by beautiful flowering hydrangeas.

"Thank you, darling."

"I'll wait up for you," Stella whispered urgently when they reached the front door.

"No need."

"I won't get a wink of sleep if I don't." Stella was in no mood to take no for an answer.

In the car their bodies were very tense. The whole situation felt indescribably dangerous. He didn't say a word other than murmur a taut, "Good evening." She nodded a silent reply. Things went very quiet after that. It all spelled out a kind of fraught hostility. Surely that was entirely reasonable for her, the abandoned one? What on earth was his problem? She was angered by the sheer irrationality, the injustice of it all. She drove on without speaking.

It had to be her day for finding parking. There was just one spot left in the restaurant's private car park beside a very impressive Maserati. She knew who owned it, a very flashy playboy who had taken an awfully long time to take a firm no for an answer.

Inside the elegant dining room with its floor-to-ceiling windows, all was soft opulence, under gleaming down lights. Tonight's palette was palest gold. Floor-skimming gold tablecloths covered the circular tables, with matching steepled napkins. Gold-rimmed wine glasses. A glass vial held a perfect single yellow rose. The comfortable chairs surrounding the tables were upholstered in an aubergine silk velvet that blended in with any number of the colour changes that occurred with the settings. Cate had been to the restaurant countless times before. She was well known to the staff and maître d'.

"*Buona sera*, Ms Hamilton, how lovely to see you."

"*Buona sera, Carlo.*"

Such a lovely smile. A man would do anything to be the recipient of such a smile. A seasoned giver of compliments, the Italian maître d' meant what he said. He wasn't surprised to see Ms Hamilton with an extremely handsome male escort. Unknown to him, which was unusual. He thought he knew just about everyone in society. But such a beautiful woman would naturally be accompanied by a man of distinction. This one he totally approved of. He had a veritable *stile di un principe*

The way he held himself! He stood a full head over Ms Hamilton, who was wearing stunning stilettos. They were an eye-riveting pair: the young woman so blonde, the man, so tall, with a fine head of hair gleaming like jet but with extraordinary blue eyes. Almost the electric blue of the male peacock's plumage, the maître d' thought fancifully. At any rate they looked so arresting they turned heads.

A bottle of white wine was settled on. No thought of champagne. No lively conversation. This wasn't a celebration. No romantic little interlude. The handsome young Italian waiter in his cropped white jacket sped away.

"So?"

"I do not want to talk about the past, Julian," she said, sounding ultra-controlled. This wasn't the incredibly exciting, incredibly passionate Ashe she had known. Even the beautiful, maddeningly upper-class English voice had hardened into tempered steel. Shades of his dear mother. Even men could turn into their mothers.

"Of course you don't," he conceded. "They tell me you have a child, a boy."

She swallowed down the flare of panic. Surely Hugh hadn't told him that? "Yes I do," she said. Her voice sounded perfectly normal.

"But no husband?"

"I'm fascinated you're interested. What about you? Wife, children, an heir to the title, *noblesse oblige* and all that?"

"My life is *my* business, Catrina." He looked straight at her.

"And so is mine," she said sharply, drawing back a little. "Shall we leave it at that?"

"How old is your boy?" His intense gaze pinned her in place. It didn't make him happy to see she had grown even more beautiful over the years, confident, polished, beautifully dressed, understated, perfect. A very assured woman.

Cate drew breath. There was no option but to lie. "Five," she said, holding his gaze, but a rose glow had entered her cheeks. "He's the love of my life."

"What about the father?" He continued to study her, this enigma that was the girl he had fallen crazily in love with. Love made such fools of people. The great and the good. It ruined careers, damaged lives, sometimes irrevocably. He hadn't really known that girl. Nor the woman. "What was he?" he asked. "Live-in lover?"

She didn't answer.

"Live out, then? With your boy. You had to consider him?"

"Hard to say what he was really." She shrugged a nonchalant shoulder. "He didn't pass the test at any rate. Look, the waiter is returning with the wine." Her gaze shifted over his shoulder.

"That sounds like the truth." He gave a brief laugh. "It's mythology in a way. Suitors being required to pass a series of tests. I've never figured out which one I failed," he said, openly contemptuous. "She's gone, she's gone, she's gone, she's gone!" He crooned it, low voiced, like a melancholy love song.

Her physical reactions were involuntary, unstoppable. Dopamine, she thought. The brain's motivational chemical. The sight and sound of him gave her enormous pleasure, an erotic rush. She wasn't entirely responsible. The man was devastating. Devastatingly handsome, devastatingly charismatic, devastatingly rich and important. Devastation all round. She knew now she had never been healed. What she had to do was push her memories further and further behind her. "Can we drop this?" She looked the picture of perfect confidence, but she was churning inside.

Cool it! her inner voice warned her.

God, she was trying to but she was using up every scrap of control.

"I don't like talking about it either." He was perilously close to bluntness, but at just the right moment he had to turn in his chair to acknowledge the waiter, who made a little business of showing the excellent Australian Riesling. It rated high

on a world list. A little was poured for sampling.
Cate was never sure if the ritual was absolutely
necessary.

Consequently she took no notice. It was a relief to study the menu, although stress had robbed
her of all appetite. Same old lethal sexual attraction; same old primitive physical responses. Could
nothing kill them? If she knew nothing could—as
in outside anyone's control—she might feel a little
better about herself.

But her brain decided to kick in. *You're pathetic.*
She sought to whip up a degree of self-disgust.
One would have thought betrayal would have been
a huge incentive. Betrayal killed every time. Only
it was impossible for them to be strangers. He was
the father of her child. Their lives were mired.
Cate turned her face away, acknowledging a female acquaintance who was staring over with avid
interest. Dinner dates were a very public matter
in city society. No hand-holding with this one. No
melting glances across the table.

What, then? Let the curious figure it out.

One course after the other arrived, each looking
like a work of art. The Japanese chef was a celeb-
rity. The lobster was superb. It settled her stomach slightly. But it was impossible to relax. She
had a life. Her son had anchored her to the earth.

She had to shield herself and her little son from all harm. Julian couldn't know about him.

"But, darling girl, why call him Julian?"

It was Stella smoothing the damp hair away from her tear-stained, exhausted face.

"I don't know," she had wailed.

Eventually Stella stopped asking.

But Julian Arnold Hamilton it was.

Coffee. Both declined a liqueur. It was then she finally asked, "Who told you about me?" There was more than a hint of aggression in her voice.

"About you?" he asked, settling his coffee cup onto the saucer. His thick black eyelashes were pointing down towards his prominent cheekbones. Jules had inherited those eyes and lashes. Abruptly he glanced up.

"Please," she said, fighting the urge to get up and run away.

"A devoted colleague." His reply was sardonic. "That Stiller woman. I gather you and she are rivals in the workplace?"

She could barely speak. "The rivalry is all on Murphy's side."

He spread his elegant hands. "Okay. I knew that. I'm not stupid. She's not only jealous of your abilities. She's jealous of your relationship with Saunders."

She was taken aback. "Hugh is my boss," she said icily.

"Fine. But he wants you, you know."

That was a truth she didn't want to know. "Then he's got a big problem," she said, coolly. "Apart from being my boss, he's old enough to be my father. And a married man. Murphy has a sick way with her. When did you see her, anyway?"

His blue eyes glinted. "For a few moments after you took off. Apparently she thought I would find the fact you're a single mother interesting."

"God alone knows why she thought that," she said, shocked by Murphy's enmity towards her. Thank God Murphy had never laid eyes on Jules. None of them had.

"Perhaps she's one of those people who can spot sparks between two people?" he suggested, very smoothly. "Sometimes there's no way of hiding our sparks. And our sorrows. That's of course if one can *feel* sorrow. Can you, Catrina?"

Some note in his voice sent a shiver down her spine. "It's hard for you to accept, isn't it, that I walked away from you?"

"You did better than that." His retort was crisp. "You *flew*. There one moment. Gone the next."

For a moment she forgot where she was. "What else could I do after that little chat with your mum?" she asked fiercely, instantly regretting her loss of control.

His black brows came together. "What little chat?" His tone bit.

"Nothing to do with *you*," she lied and waved a nonchalant hand.

"I'd like to know."

"Nothing *to* know," she clipped off. "If you're ready, I would like to leave. This was a business dinner, after all. I've told you Lady McCready is happy to meet with you. I need to accompany you but we can handle that. You can take it from there. We're both adults. There's no need whatsoever for her to know we've met before."

"Meet? Is that what we did?" His voice had taken on a decided edge. "You obviously have no trouble burying memories."

"You had no difficulty coming out of it, either," she said. "Lady McCready will be sure to ask you something about yourself and your family. I didn't ask after your mother. How is she?"

His eyes turned as cold as an iceberg. "You're actually interested?"

"Only possibly."

"She was bitterly disappointed in you."

"Blimey!" she said facetiously, gathering up her satin and brass-studded evening clutch. "That's mothers for you. Shall we go?" But there was fear in her. And a sudden confusion. But that was just Alicia protecting herself. Alicia had always had her own agenda.

"Certainly." He put up a hand signalling their waiter, who hurried over.

"I'll pay for this," Cate said, her credit card already in hand. This was business. She could claim.

"You *will* pay, Catrina, but not for dinner," he said. His bluer than blue eyes held her to him.

Captive.

For a moment she damn near crumpled.

Stella was waiting up just as she had promised. Stella was a woman who would go to any lengths to protect her little family. Cate. Jules. Herself. She was a protective person and she had proved it. Hadn't she gone to extraordinary lengths to protect her little sister? She had devoted her life to the interests of others, Annabel, then Cate. Like mother, like daughter, both fallen pregnant though she had avoided sitting in judgment. And there was darling little Jules. Occasionally all her self-sacrifice, her stress on the importance of family, had put easy-going Arnold's nose right out of joint.

I took on this job, Arnold.

Now you're stuck with it. I'm stuck with it. We're stuck with it. Or are you really, Stella?

Always those searching looks from Arnold as if he sought to put a huge dent in her armour but couldn't quite bring it off.

"Give it to me straight." Stella took Cate's arm, leading her into the living room where down lights cast a golden glow. Through the sliding glass doors onto the balcony across the multicoloured sequinned waters Sydney's great landmarks, the Bridge and the Opera House, lit up the night.

"I think I'll have a drink first," Cate said, going in search of one.

"What?"

"I need a drink. Trust me." Cate headed to the kitchen, Stella following, a pleat of concern etched into her forehead. She was wearing a luxurious nightgown with a matching robe, which she pulled tight in a fit of nerves. "Join me?" Cate held up a bottle of cognac.

"I have a feeling I might need to," Stella returned crisply.

"Besides, it will make you sleep better." Cate poured a shot into two crystal balloons. They went back into the living room and settled into two armchairs. Only then did Cate begin to relate economically the events of the evening while Stella sat with folded hands...

"What did that Murphy Stiller think she was gaining telling him you had a son?' Stella rolled out her anger. On the odd occasion Stella was seriously formidable.

"Unsure. Murphy has her own agenda. He did ask how old my son was. Of course I lied. Had to. I said he was five." Cate ran her tongue around her lips, tasting fine brandy.

"And he never said a thing about his own family? I would have thought he would. Are you keeping something from me?"

"Nary a word." Cate shook her blonde head while thinking, *You certainly did.* "His father was always a no-go area with the whole family."

"I can understand that. Much too painful." Geoffrey Carlisle, recruited from Oxford into the British Security Service—MI5 or MI6, no one seemed to know—had been killed by a militant's bullet in the Middle East where he was touring. That was years back. He was a highly intelligent man and a polyglot; the Middle East had been his speciality area. Had he lived it was he who would have inherited the title Baron Wyndham, not his son.

"He told me his life is his business," Cate said. "Our meeting was business, not a rehash of old times. I did, however, ask after his mother."

Stella's expression froze. "Was that wise?"

"Confound them all," said Cate, polishing off her drink. "Don't worry, Stell. I can handle this."

"Surely there's someone else who can go with him, introduce him to Lady McCready?" Stella felt a great surge of anxiety. She wondered if her niece had the strength to resist the man who had ripped her heart out. It didn't feel that way.

Cate gave a crooked smile. "I could suggest Murphy. She took to him at first sight. Turned into a positive sunbeam. Ask anyone." She laughed, then abruptly sobered. "No, Stell, I have to do it.

Hugh expects it. Show commitment. Integral part of the team and all that. I just have to get it over with. He'll buy his island retreat. He'll invest in our mineral wealth, then he'll go home. Back to what's important to him." Her eyes frosted over. "I could of course lead him on. What do you think?" Her laugh held black humour. "The physical attraction is still there. Can't kill it. Fact of life. I don't think I'd have all that much trouble coaxing him into the palm of my hand," she said with contempt. "Just think of it!" she crowed.

"I don't *want* to think of it," Stella said, her jaw clenched. "Now is not the time to play with fire. Sacrifice everything we've built up."

Cate waved her brandy balloon in the air, not really hearing. Stella sometimes did set the calm image aside. "I could tell him to get lost. Reverse process if you like. Put *him* on the rack."

"Don't even think of going there," Stella warned, unable to control a shudder. Cate had never been cured of Julian Carlisle. That was at the heart of it all. Cate was only in remission. Stella felt a savage anger.

CHAPTER FOUR

LADY MCCREADY HAD readied herself for their visit. She had made it her business to go around the island in her cute little go-cart, driven by her faithful Davey, who managed just about everything for her. His wife, Mary, did the cooking and the housework. She was well looked after and she looked after her staff, her friends, really.

It was a glorious day, the sky a cloudless azure blue. Bluer yet the sparkling sea. The green lawns were mown to perfection, fringed with alternate borders of agapanthus in blue and white. There were sculptural beds of strelitzias and agaves, numerous types of hibiscus, marvellous tree ferns, pandanus and of course the soaring palms, their fronds swaying gently in the breeze. As they swept past, the scent of ginger blossom and gardenia spiked the air. Davey was a zealous and talented gardener. He had turned the island retreat into a botanical garden with his imaginative mix of exotic and endemic plants.

Lady McCready brushed a snowy strand of hair off her high forehead. "Such a lovely cooling breeze, Davey."

"That it is. I'm looking forward to meeting your guest, a lord and all. Miss Hamilton, of course, I've met. She's a special young lady."

"She is that." Lady McCready had taken an instant liking to Catrina. Not only was she a lovely-looking young woman, but she was kind with a quick intuition. "I know Catrina will have our best interests at heart. You and Mary are very dear to me, Davey. You've always made us proud." As ever Lady McCready included her beloved late husband as though he were still there. She fully intended telling Lord Wyndham part of any deal they might strike would include a clause stating Davey and Mary were to remain on the island for as long as they wished. Isla Bella had been home to them for over twenty years. They would make perfect caretakers. They loved the island as much as she did. She had provided for them in her will. Which was as it should be.

They had taken the morning flight from Sydney to Townsville, then twenty minutes later boarded the launch *Petrel* for the trip to the island. The only access was by boat or helicopter. Wyndham held her hand tightly while she moved rather perilously into the launch that was swinging away from the jetty on the high tide. Again contact was like being plugged into a million volts. She would have to avoid it. He was casually dressed, beige chinos, tan leather belt, short-sleeved, open-necked blue cotton shirt, a wide-brimmed cream straw hat, slouched on one side. Sunglasses in his breast pocket. He looked extremely handsome, perfectly at ease.

She had dressed casually as well. All virgin white. White cotton-denim jeans, white shirt, added a fancy snakeskin belt, leather and canvas bag over her shoulder, Gucci sunglasses on her nose, her long hair tied back with a silk scarf that matched the vibrant yellows and reds in her bag. Both wore sensible albeit stylish shoes.

"No need to be nervous," he mocked. "I wasn't going to let you fall."

"I don't believe you."

"Really?" His tone bit.

"Well, I have caught the odd flicker of hostility. God knows why."

"Catrina, you would have to be joking," he drawled.

She felt caught in the *thrust* of it all, translated the momentary sense of powerlessness into a brilliant smile. "The captain is looking our way."

"Probably wondering what's going on." He nodded to the captain, a good-looking bearded man some forty odd years, as spick and span as his boat. The owner nodded back.

They were under way, heading eastward to Isla Bella, a continental island some six nautical miles from the mainland. She peered down into the water. It had gone from aqua to turquoise, deepening into cobalt the further they moved away from the quay. It wasn't going to be a placid run. The trade wind was chasing them.

"Any sharks around?" he asked after a while.

"Why don't you chance it?" she suggested, almost cheerfully.

"I'd make sure I pulled you in." The look on his dark face was a bit scary.

"You're a prince," she remarked.

"Not I."

"No, you're a lord. I bet you revel in it?"

"Well, it can make one's passage through life a little easier," he admitted. "This is a very beautiful part of the world." He spoke in conversational style, maybe for the captain's benefit. "Of course the Great Barrier Reef is one of the world's natural wonders."

She played her part. She couldn't help but notice the owner of the launch *had* been fixing them with a speculative eye. "It's the great breakwater that protects hundreds of kilometres of our eastern seaboard and the continental islands. Isla Bella is a continental island, as I told you. It has a rather steeply sloping hill cutting down the middle. The house is on the leeward side—"

"Needless to say," he interjected smoothly.

She continued like a tour guide. "There are volcanic islands, coral islands, some with extensive fringing reefs, cays, hundreds of them. I hope you know about our cyclones," she said with a warning in her voice. "Most years they're spawned in the Coral Sea before they eventually cross the Queensland coast. We had horrific Yasi at the beginning of 2011. The largest and most powerful cyclone to hit Queensland in living memory. It wreaked havoc. There was a phenomenal amount of flooding. Thousands left homeless. The whole state was affected. Parts of Brisbane went under."

"It did make world news," he pointed out gently. "From what I've seen and heard you're well into the recovery process."

"True. The entire country got behind Queensland and the areas of Victoria that were flood affected. There was enormous community spirit."

"And Isla Bella?"

"Mercifully it was spared," she said, visualising the old TV flood coverage. "Although a couple of the tourist islands weren't. Lady McCready and her staff actually stayed on the island right through. I believe there's a cyclone-proof bunker."

"That's good to know," he said wryly.

"Not putting you off?" She ventured a sideways glance. She had tried *everything* to forget him. Now she was up to her neck in it again.

"Are you trying to?"

"Simply want you to understand. There are risks to be considered."

"Which I'm well acquainted with. Hurricanes affect the Bahamas as well as many other countries in the world. I could have sworn I told you all about Hurricane Noel in the late nineties when my family was there."

She shrugged. "Don't recall." Why admit to any memories at all? Hadn't Stella perfected it? "Still own property there, do you?"

"Yes, as a matter of fact. But I'm looking for a less accessible holiday retreat. I'm hoping Isla Bella is a good choice."

"How about a little more information? How many children do you have—three or four?"

"To your one?" he said, leaning on the rail and looking out over the deep blue sea mantled with silver pinpoints of light.

"Of course, you're not going to tell me."

"Why should I?" He glanced at her with eyes that luminous electric blue. "I would have thought you'd check up on me."

She had thought of it. Too many times. "Why ever would I do that?"

"Odd, I never checked up on you either," he

said. "Of course I knew I was bound to sooner or later."

Prepare yourself.

"Meaning what?" she asked, clear challenge in her voice.

"Then I thought it would be a big mistake," he admitted. "Why would I ever want to hear of you again?"

She hid the tide of anger that swept through her. "Absolutely right. I, for one, am a totally different person these days."

"You were a totally different person *then*," he returned curtly. "At least from the person I thought you were."

"Dangerous to assume you know anyone," she retorted. "We don't even know ourselves. Everything changes, that's the thing."

"Well, I'm resigned to the fact I never knew you."

"Our goals in life weren't the same." She had to breathe in deeply. What would he do, what would he say, if she told him she was the mother of his child? React with rage, toss her overboard? She knew the fact that she had kept that momentous piece of news from him would bring a forceful response. For all she knew he didn't have a son.

The wind had picked up. It suddenly seized her silk scarf, wrenching it from her head. She made a wild grab for it. It was a lovely scarf. Hermes.

He lunged for it too, executing some manoeuvre that had him rescuing the scarf while capturing her pivoting body in a powerful one-armed grip. They slammed into one another.

Heat scorched her body. It burnt holes in her character that felt as weak as her arms and her legs. Deep, dark emotions were swirling through her like dangerous debris. The tips of her breasts were against his chest, hard as berries with a physical response she couldn't control. What she felt was desire. Shame and guilt would follow. She thought she had wised up, grown up. Now it appeared she really hadn't.

She jerked away from him violently. She had loved him once. The man who had deceived her. "Thank you," she said, sounding more ferocious than grateful.

"No trouble." He kept watching her like a hawk.

The wind had picked up considerably, making a grab for her hair. The full length of it whipped free, a long column of blonde shining silk. "If I might venture a suggestion, leave it," he said.

For answer she put up her hands, scraping her hair back with her fingers. Long tendrils were escaping but she couldn't help that. Once more she tied the scarf, knotting it twice. "Well?" She found she couldn't bear him staring at her.

"Just for a moment you reminded me of a girl

I once knew," he said, for a moment pitched back in time. "Hard to believe it was you."

"I was very young and incredibly foolish. Let's drop it."

"Why not? What the hell!"

His private life had not fared well during the ensuing years. Not that he was about to tell her that. Inevitable she would find out eventually. His public life, his business life, had gone exceedingly well. Losing her—the way she had left— the short, pitiful letter of explanation, if that was what one could call it, had affected him deeply. No one could have been treated worse. The moment his back was turned, she had fled at frightful speed. The final indignity. Maybe she had known what she was doing from the beginning? It was he who had got it all wrong. His mother, appalled by Catrina's behaviour, had done everything in her power to console him, until finally she was forced to stop in despair.

He had chosen his own way to get through. He had used his perfectly good brain to amass a fortune over a few years. On solid evidence he was a great success, a man of property, with many possessions.

He didn't have a wife. He didn't have a son. Marina had hung in there as long as she thought there was hope. Now and again under pressure from the family, especially his mother, he had considered asking Marina to be his wife. Had he not met Catrina Hamilton who knew? He could have married Marina. She was a lovely person, eminently suitable. Marina had deserved better. She had gone on to marry a good friend of his, Simon Bolton. He had in fact been best man at the wedding. They remained close friends.

It was Catrina who had stolen his heart. She had never contacted him again. Simply vanished from his life. Once hope was gone there was only heartbreak to be endured. Women weren't the only ones to suffer that. Men did too. He had missed her. God, how he'd missed her. Hated her too. What she had done he regarded as not only cowardly but cruel. The cruellest, the most demoralising part was, there was hardly a time and a long, long night he hadn't thought of her. He could almost believe destiny had thrown them together again. For a crime there was punishment.

This time she wouldn't get off so easily. An unmarried mother said it. Catrina played games with men's minds and men's bodies. Probably nothing really touched her. Except—and he knew it in his bones—her son. Her son would be her Achilles heel. Meeting the boy might deliver a judgment. Apparently she kept him well hidden. Hugh Saunders hadn't met the boy either. But he knew where she lived. The big mystery was how had the boy's father opted out so easily? Either he had placed little value on being the father of a child, or Catrina hadn't told him.

Simply used him.

It happened. Women were getting better and better at using men.

They sat down on the loggia to a light, delicious lunch served by Lady McCready's housekeeper, Mary, a pleasant, capable woman clearly devoted to her mistress. The loggia with its series of archways faced a cerulean infinity-edged pool. Beyond that, breathtaking views of the Coral Sea. There were comfortable white furnishings set back from the pool, the tables, couches and chairs protected from the dazzling sun by large blue, white fringed umbrellas. Huge terracotta planters framed either side of the arches, filled with blossoming hibiscus in a range of brilliant colours. The house presented the classic Mediterranean style of architecture he was long familiar with.

Over lunch Lady McCready didn't bother him with personal questions. He had asked to speak to her privately regarding possible negotiations. If she was surprised she had hidden it well. Davey would take Catrina on a tour of the gardens while they talked. Catrina, however, was allowed to take him on a tour of what was the large house.

"I'm not as spry as I once was," Lady McCready said with a laugh and a little wave of her beringed hand. Indeed the regal little lady dressed in a gorgeous kaftan looked quite frail, though the years had dealt kindly with her. "I'll wait here for you."

Immediately they were out of earshot and Cate went on the attack. "So you cut me out of the negotiations? That wasn't the plan."

"Plans change," he said briefly, moving ahead of her. "I really don't need *you* to make a business pitch. I would have thought that it was obvious I can handle it myself. Lady McCready and I won't have a problem dealing with each other on what I'm sure is a seven-figure deal. It's a truly beautiful home they've created here, but I haven't yet decided whether it's irresistible to me. It's clear no expense has been spared. Isla Bella is much more than a hideaway. More like an Italianate villa. It must have taken a long time to complete the project?" He suddenly turned to her, caught her out staring at him.

"Five years, I believe." She knew she gave a betraying flush. "They commissioned an Italian architect. Lady McCready loves all things Italian. She was responsible for creating their island home. Surely you can tell me what you think so far?"

He gave an elegant shrug. "The house in the Bahamas is British West Indies style. It's lighter, more airy, minimalistic when compared with this. I suppose this could be called a grand house. It's lavishly decorated. Some might find it overwhelming. Changes would have to be made."

"Many VIPs have stayed here as guests," she pointed out stiffly, thinking he now had reservations. It wasn't what he wanted? Good. "The McCreadys were known for their lavish hospitality. Three prime ministers have stayed here. But then you would have VIP guests of your own. Who knows, even royalty might stay a day or two?"

"Okay, you can show me upstairs now." He ignored her last comment. They had seen the major rooms of the first floor. He had declined entering the housekeeper's domain, the kitchen, which Cate knew had been brought up to state of the art. Perhaps he simply wasn't interested in how kitchens worked.

They walked back into the hallway with its intricately patterned flooring featuring three types of Italian stone before taking the black wrought-iron curving staircase to the upper floor.

"Six double bedrooms all with en suites." She spoke exactly like a Realtor showing a client over a high-end property. "How many family members have you got?" Her voice was remarkably cool when inside she felt terribly unsettled. Sexual radiance came off him in waves. She made certain she didn't stand too close to catch them. Even then, the scent of him was in her nostrils, as powerful an aphrodisiac as it had ever been. She took a deep breath.

This has to stop.

"I don't think you have any right to ask," he answered in a terse, pragmatic fashion. He continued to move ahead of her, as though not caring if she followed, which she did briskly. All the bedrooms were very spacious with a series of white-shuttered French doors opening out onto a covered balcony. The master suite was the most luxurious with a huge canopied bed with white filmy bed hangings. He walked out onto the balcony and looked at the glorious view with the brilliant sun scattering diamond sparkles across the deep blue waters.

"The master suite," Cate said quite unnecessarily when he came back inside. How could she ever cancel out her memories, the two of them in bed together, the weight of his body on hers, the power of his hands, the interlocking limbs, their mouths, their tongues…the high-burning passion of it all. The way of all flesh. She had prayed for someone to come into her life to supplant him. No one had even come close. It was a savage blow, but she had been adjusting to it. She had her son. Not everyone found their soul mate.

Had Cate only known it, Wyndham was thinking much the same thing. The excitement, the heat, the enormous pleasure he had taken even in their clashes, too little time before they had been thrown headlong into love making. She had touched his body, his heart, his mind and his soul. He had thought things would never change. How wrong could a man be? The merry dance she had led him went nowhere? To hell? Even now, God help him, he wanted to bolt the door, throw her down on the bed, make punishing love to her. She had known all about passion. About giving herself to a man. The merest contact with her had brought back the past.

Yet when he spoke his voice was coolly casual. "I think that does it. Enjoy your trip around the garden. They look splendid, by the way. Such a pity you never did get to see the full restoration of Radclyffe Hall's gardens."

"I did what I wanted to do," she said, her tone tight. "I got away."

The question was, what was she going to do now?

Just the sight of him and the years had melted away.

The buggy ride around the gardens was a pleasure. It even shifted her mind off what was going on inside the house. Davey had packed the leeward side of the island with dozens of species of native plants that required minimal watering. An astonishing array of agaves caught her eye, some with pearly marking. There were striking aloes with yellow flowers and millions of hot pink and bright yellow little succulent flowers. Davey seemed to welcome her interest in the garden he had created out of what was once a wilderness.

Wyndham didn't need her. He was the billionaire potential buyer. It hadn't taken her long to see Lady McCready both liked and trusted him. Lord Julian Wyndham was a very charming man. He had certainly made the old lady's eyes twinkle. No problem with an *à deux*, then. Amazing Lady McCready hadn't asked him a single question about his private life. He had acted as if he didn't have one.

When she returned to the house it was obvious the meeting had gone well. Lady McCready's soft powdery cheeks were flushed with pleasure. *Catrina has justified my faith in her,* Lady McCready thought. She had brought her the right person to buy the island. Lord Wyndham would treat it like a second home. Now wasn't that a wonderful outcome? She didn't tell Catrina. Julian—he had insisted she call him Julian—had asked her to give him a little more time before they made their announcement. In return he would allow Catrina to have a contract drawn up. Rather than wanting Davey and Mary off the island, he was delighted they would stay on as caretakers.

* * *

The launch returned for them mid-afternoon, with the sun casting a glittery veil of light over water as blue as a precious stone. Cate was glad she didn't suffer from motion sickness because the sea was unusually choppy, more so than on the run over to the island. She started for the shelter of the cabin not long after they boarded, her skin dewed with fine spray. She took a couple of tissues out of her tote bag, gently mopping her face. He was still out braced against the rail. She was reminded he was a good sailor. Or so he had said, though she was sure it was true. They had never got around to the trip to Cornwall they had planned, but he had shown her a photograph of the family yacht, *Calliope IV*, long and sleek as any luxury automobile, all varnished mahogany that gleamed even in the photograph, a golden mast tall enough to reach the cloudy sky.

The rocky passage tested her. The diesel fumes were making her feel sick. She would be glad when they reached the mainland. He had asked her if she was okay before going off to speak to the launch owner. She heard the owner laugh out loud a few times, genuinely amused. Again she remembered he could be really funny, witty and entertaining. He had been spoilt rotten by his mother and his sisters, Olivia and Leonie, both older, both endowed with beauty, who adored him. She supposed his sisters—strangely enough she had got on well with them—were married as well. Probably with children. There had been plenty of young men in their lives. Part of his close-knit family who no doubt would be visitors to Isla Bella if he bought it.

So far no commitment.

The launch slid smooth and easy into dock. An exchange of handshakes with the captain before they moved off.

"Sure you're okay?" For a minute he sounded genuinely concerned. "You've gone very pale." Her satin-smooth skin had lost colour.

"I'm fine," she said testily. "The diesel fumes were getting to me."

"And you haven't found your land legs."

"Don't you believe it." She pulled away from his steadying arm, her body as poised and alert as a dancer's. "We can catch a taxi back to the hotel, or we can walk."

"Up to you." He shrugged. "I'd like to look around. What are those beautiful trees?" he asked, looking towards an avenue of them. "The flowers look like frangipani, but the leaves don't."

"Evergreens," she said. "They're a species of frangipani. As you can see the flowers are a pure white. They grow prolifically up here. I saw a whole grove of them on the island. Davey is a wonderful gardener. He and Mary have a blissful lifestyle. I believe Lady McCready required a clause in any contract to state they remain on the island for as long as they want."

"I believe so," he said, not to be drawn any further.

CHAPTER FIVE

THE BEDSIDE PHONE rang with a startling shrillness.

"Yes," she said briefly, focusing on pulling the bath robe together. She'd barely had time to get out of the shower.

"Wyndham." His voice was quiet, impassive. "I assume you intend to eat?"

A heart-stopping moment. She gave a tiny cough as though clearing her throat. "I thought I'd have something in my room."

She heard his exasperated sigh. "Don't be so damned ridiculous. I'm told there's an excellent restaurant within walking distance, the Blue Lotus."

"I'm in no mood for dinner. With *you*," she added. Perched on the side of the bed she was feeling all of a sudden stricken. She should complain to God for allowing him back into her life again. How could God be so cruel?

He gave you free will.

"My dear Catrina, you're supposed to keep me

happy," he answered smoothly. "Isn't that what your boss told you? We need to keep him happy until he comes on board?"

"So this is blackmail?"

"Blackmail is fine with me. Saunders is your boss. He was speaking to one of his senior staff. He only had praise for you. Don't disappoint him. I'll call for you at seven-thirty." He hung up.

She had two options. Not answer the door. Or get dressed. Hugh had thrown her head first into the thickets. It was a dark picture she had of herself. A sad, permanently love-struck woman. A woman whose whole mission had been to forget one man. And dismally failed.

"We're a crazy lot, aren't we?" She addressed the woman in the bathroom mirror.

Better believe it! her reflection replied.

She could behave very badly, be provocative, try to seduce him. She had hinted as much to Stella who had been appalled. But there would be some satisfaction in playing that game. Only he was a married man. And after all these years he still had enormous power to hurt her. Besides, the past had a way of repeating itself. She had asked for what she got. She had paid the price. Accepted responsibility.

Wyndham was untouchable.

* * *

When she was dressed she knew she looked good.
She liked looking good. A woman needed every
aid in the arsenal. On impulse she had packed a
resort-style maxi dress by a well-known Australian designer famous for her kaftans and resort
wear. The floral-printed silk was beautiful, a luscious collection of tropical blooms. The light green
tracery of leaves picked up the colour of her eyes.
She left her hair long and loose when her inten-
tions had been to pull it back.

Maybe you're just losing it?

Fair enough! A woman was allowed to lose it
now and then.

They had a table facing the promenade and the
beach beyond. He looked absurdly handsome, absurdly sexy, so tall and lean with his dark hair
and intensely blue eyes. He had even picked up a
tan. It gave her an involuntary shock of pleasure
just looking at him. What she needed was vigilant
self-management. He was wearing a teal-coloured
open-necked linen shirt with tiny pearly white but-
tons, the long sleeves turned back, navy jeans.
He looked great. The young waitress thought so
too. Not even close to hiding it. When he gave her
his heart-lurching smile, colour flamed into her
cheeks. No question—a great smile was a fantastic weapon.

She heard herself agreeing to an entrée, a tar-

tare of ocean trout garnished with salmon roe, for the mains, steamed Reef Red Emperor served in a banana leaf with a papaya, chilli and coconut salsa. All local products, the seafood caught that very day, the hovering waitress assured them. Cate sat back allowing him to choose a crisp New Zealand sauvignon blanc to go with the meal. The whole thing felt like an exquisite piece of theatre. Two people hostile to each other but maintaining an urbane façade.

The restaurant was a far cry from the elegance of C'est Bon. It was unpretentious, but very clean and attractive, above all welcoming. They were fortunate to get a table because the large open room was near full. She heard a mix of languages from the enthusiastic diners at the other tables: Japanese, Chinese, German and Italian and, she thought, Taiwanese. The colour blue set the tone. Unusual blue lighting, blue and white candy-striped tablecloths, comfortable white painted chairs. A lovely creamy conch-shell centre table held an exquisite blue water lily positioned atop its emerald-green pad.

He glanced up at the lighting over the small bar with real interest. "They did a study fairly recently on colour and the effect it has on us. One of our leading London architects designed the experimental blue lighting in a new restaurant. Far more usual to see red, but the blue worked wonders apparently. Diners came *alive* at around ten p.m. It was as though their body clocks had been reset. They stayed much later into the evening too. Drank more. Never tried it myself."

She had to make a contribution. "They tried much the same experiment with the colour red. Professional footballers were given either a red or a blue jersey to wear in a game. Those wearing the red jerseys not only felt more confident of a win—their own explanation—they did win."

"Well, the theory can be demonstrated tonight," he suggested, the curve of his mouth frankly mocking.

"I can promise you it won't be a late night for me," she answered repressively.

"Why so anxious to get rid of me?" he asked with mock humour. "Surely I'm someone from the old days? A one-time boyfriend? I mean, it wasn't as though you were fixated on me."

She turned her blonde head away, exposing a sculpted jaw line and throat. "That wasn't the plan."

"What was the plan? Two-timing someone at home?" A hardness had entered his voice.

"A variety of reasons," she said.

"All tainted."

"Nothing could have been further from my mind. Can we keep the focus on the present," she said firmly.

"By all means. Why can't you say my name?"

He was exerting far too much pressure. "I don't trust myself to."

"Meaning?" Baffled, he stared into her eyes, not knowing what the hell she was talking about.

Why can't you keep your mouth shut? the voice inside her head cut in.

"It was good to walk away from you, Ashe. Good to walk away from your family, England."

"When my family liked you so much?" Anger hit him. "You just pulled the plug on all of us?"

His sisters had really liked her. She had liked them. They had treated her like a friend, respected her and her opinions. Briefly they had touched her life. His mother? Another story. Memories of Alicia would stay with her for ever. She would always feel that backlash of rejection. It was a wonder Marina had been considered good enough for her son. "Surely it can't be of any importance any more," she said, with no emotion in her voice.

Provoked, he suddenly caught her hand across the table, his fingers very tight on hers. "You claimed you *loved* me."

Denial was impossible. "Oh, for God's sake!" *Betray nothing.*

Only he wouldn't let her fingers go. That mystical clasp of their hands! She had to suck in her breath. She was no better at controlling her responses now than she had been years ago.

"You inherited your Gothic pile, the title, Marina, the Earl's daughter, Radclyffe Hall. Wasn't that enough?"

"Not Gothic at all as you very well know," he returned shortly. "What the hell are you hiding, Catrina?" His black brows drew together, making him look extraordinarily formidable.

"And I suppose you're so up front?" she retaliated, still keeping her voice low. "We've been thrown into this situation. I'm not enjoying it any more than you."

"Brave words, but what's the reality?" he challenged. "Your hand is trembling."

"That's because you've got my fingers wedged tight."

"No, I haven't."

"Look," she said in what she hoped was a conciliatory manner. "Don't let's have a spat in public. We'll finish up, then walk back to the hotel." It was much too dangerous to stay within his orbit. "I gather I might become privy to an announcement some time tomorrow so we can head back. No doubt you've told Lady McCready all about yourself and your illustrious family. You can't help looking and acting very grand. Lady McCready would like that. A mega-hero."

"Please, no fake admiration. It's just a waste of time. I have no doubt of your powers, Catrina, and I'm speaking from experience, but it appears all you can offer a man is delusion."

"Takes one to know one."

He had been busy finding his credit card but his dark head shot up. "What did you say?"

"I'm just going with the flow, Ashe." Her green eyes beneath their naturally dark brows were enigmatic.

Sexual attraction was hell, he thought. No way to get rid of it. "Know what I think? You're still playing tricks," he returned with a lick of contempt. "You started out that way as a girl. You've kept going."

She was rattled, but managed coolly, "The short answer is, not with a married man. That's a no-go zone."

"*Is* it? What about the man who fathered your child? I have to say I feel sorry for the guy. Did you even tell him you were pregnant?"

Her control almost slipped. "That's the tricky part," she said, tossing a long lock of her hair over her shoulder. "Write me off, Ashe."

Just like you wrote me.

On the way back to the hotel he had to rescue her again. She had stepped off the pavement precipitously; a second later a car window was wound down and a young male voice bawled at her, "Yoo-hoo, blondie, are you trying to get yourself killed? You can get in if you like."

Heads swivelled everywhere. Wyndham grabbed hold of her and smartly waved the young driver on. She was staggering now under the rush of adrenaline, dry-mouthed with fright. She had stepped off the pavement looking right but not left, the reason being *he* was to her left. She had made it clear she hadn't wanted him to take her arm. The bad news was, she was such a mass of leaping nerves she hadn't been paying sufficient attention to the road or indeed anything much. The traffic was by no means heavy. Couples were strolling arm in arm enjoying the balmy breeze but the beetle-sized vehicle approaching the corner would have come close to collecting her only for Wyndham.

A dead silence lasted for several seconds. "As the kid said, are you trying to get yourself killed?" he snapped. He sounded deeply angry.

"Hey, don't get excited. Nothing happened."

He didn't buy that. "Come on." His retort was sharp. "Your heart is hammering."

He would know. His arm was pressed over it. "Well, you see the problem, don't you? You're manhandling me."

"You *need* manhandling," he said, abruptly releasing her.

She said nothing. She was so shocked she was able to maintain a spurious air of total calm. They set off again, but this time he kept a light hold on her arm. She didn't protest. Her brain wasn't working yet.

Back at the hotel he walked along the empty corridor, stopping first at her door. His room was further down.

This is your chance to self-destruct.

"Goodnight," she said rapidly, her agitation evident. What she had here was a major departure from her rational, ordered life.

"What on earth's the problem?" He stared down into her overwrought face. The first time he had seen vulnerability from the Frost Queen. Oddly enough it hurt him.

"Okay, I feel a bit shaky," she admitted. "If you hadn't pulled me back I could have been injured." It was Jules she was thinking about. She had to stay safe and well for her son.

"*Would* have been," he corrected. "You're pale enough to pass out." Indeed her creamy skin had lost colour. "You want a slug of something. Come to that, I need one too." He felt like a man standing on a cliff with his feet halfway over. She wasn't worth loving. She never had been. But by God she was more of a threat than ever. She still possessed her powerful sexual allure in spades. He didn't *need* her love any more. But he was mad to take her to bed. The surest way to move on. Taking her to bed was a strategy of sorts. Finally get her out of his system.

He took the entry card out of her nerveless hand, opening the door, waiting a moment for her to precede him. She had such grace in her movements. Her lovely subtle perfume was in his nostrils. He even knew it. Chanel. He was the one who had actually introduced her to Chanel, buying her perfume along with a dozen and more Christmas presents all packaged up beautifully, the card bearing her name. Those were the days when he was just Julian Ashton Carlisle with no idea a peerage was waiting for him. That honour should have been for his beloved father, a hero in many people's eyes, not just his family's.

"Ashe, this is—" She broke off, unable to find the right words.

"Madness?" he asked. The black humour of it overtook him and he began to laugh.

"Leave now." She was in near despair.

"It would be a very good idea, but let's have a drink first. Settle the nerves." Settle the feelings that threatened to become overwhelming. He went to where the drinks were kept.

"I'll go splash water on my face," she announced.

"Might as well," he said, as laconic as any Aussie.

She returned after about five minutes, feeling a bit closer to normal.

He on the other hand looked as though he had zipped back into top gear. "You look better," he said casually. She looked exquisite. But she had lost the ultra-control he had seen from her. "Recovered?"

"I didn't actually fall apart, did I?" she shot back.

"You could have fooled me." He passed her a glass containing a small measure of whisky.

"Cheers," she said idiotically and drank it down, shuddering a little as the fiery spirits kicked in. Her capacity for controlling herself was stretched so far it was about to snap. "Thank you for tonight. But time to go," she said with determination, before she was drawn even further into the whirlpool.

"I know that. I know if I were in my right mind I'd have steered clear of you."

"What a relief it is to hear you say that."

You breaker of hearts.

"Only exposure to you has quite clouded my better judgment."

"Well, it hasn't clouded mine. What I told you is true. Married men are in the no-go zone."

"As though I believe it," he scoffed. "You'd have married men falling over one another with insatiable desire. Look at poor old Saunders."

"I'm not happy to hear you call my boss 'poor old Saunders.'"

"I'll be glad to call him 'poor old Hugh Saunders, CEO Inter-Austral' if you like. Give me your hand."

"Sorry. Holding hands with you is way down my list."

"Whatever did you see in me? No, seriously, I want to know."

"It was like a switch was turned. On. Off. You know how it goes."

"Catrina, that's wicked," he condemned her. "Seriously wicked. No one has the right to deliberately break the heart of someone who cares for them."

She stared at him in amazement, then snapped, "Destroyed by grief, were you? How long after did you get married?"

Something was all wrong, he thought. The expression in her crystal-clear green eyes was haunted. How could that be? It was the moment to come clean and tell her he and Marina had never tied the knot. That had been his mother's grand design. But why should he answer head-on and expose himself to even more humiliation? She would find out soon enough.

Cate waved the question off. "Hey, no need to tell me. Wedding of the year, was it?" There was a definite giddiness in her head. "Please go, Ashe." She made an effusive gesture towards the door.

Mockery was in his glittering eyes. "See you for breakfast?"

She laid her palms against her ears. "Never!"

"How about coffee? I'll have Lady McCready's answer by tomorrow afternoon."

"Coffee will be fine," she bit off. "We'll have it at the airport."

She went to move past him, but as she did so his arm encircled her waist. That was the trigger. Immediately she was engulfed in fire as her flesh came into contact with his. She could feel the searing glow on her skin. She could feel the blood pumping in and out of her heart. Surely he could hear the loud beat? For a shocking moment she actually leaned against him, *compelled* to, assailed by memories so vivid they could never be erased.

At a touch, I yield.

"So the seduction scene," he murmured, blatant cynicism in his voice. "Who planned it, you or me?" His arm tightened.

"None of it was ever planned." She twisted her body away from him.

Something inexplicable was in her tone. It frustrated him immensely. He swung her fully into his arms, more roughly than he intended. For all he knew she could be in some way deranged. "Look, I'm not following you at all," he cried with more than a hint of desperation. He stared into her trans-

lucent green eyes that hid so much. "Is this your
on-and-off stunt? If it is, *stop* it."

"Pray it isn't!" Masses of her long blonde hair
had fallen back. At this moment of extreme upset
the very worst thing could happen. It lured her as
much as frightened her.

The promise of her was too lavish for him.

The rush was headlong.

His mouth on hers. Call him a fool, but this was
what he wanted. This helpless, hopeless admis-
sion of need.

It blitzed all rational thought. Her full mouth
was luscious, a magnet for his. Their tongues
flickered briefly, coiled in a dance of love to some
hypnotising rhythm. Cate's eyelids fluttered shut.
There was no tenderness to their kiss. Rather, raw
passion, a kind of anger, like a two-edged sword.
What had started off as a moment of shock rapidly
turned to intense physical pleasure. But even the
extravagant passion of kissing couldn't satisfy the
deep hunger, the force of it that shook them. She
could never mistake any other man for Ashe. No
other man could arouse such feelings. No other
man could be so addictive.

She was hooked. Her love-starved body wanted
more and more of him.

He hauled her right up against him, his hands
slipping down over her, warm and strong, The
hardness of his arousal pressing urgently into her

cleft. The miraculous feel of her body against his! Would he never stop wanting her? He hadn't been able to erase the memories. She had buried herself deep in his psyche, locking him in with a golden key.

Now they were totally absorbed, the one in the other. The pleasure was ravishing. Cate's body felt full to the brim of it. There had never been anything measured in their love-making. It had always been total. She was a one-man woman. That was the reality she had to face. Only she couldn't allow him to see it. This could be written off as an aberration; an overwhelmingly powerful sexual attraction. No more to it than that. She had to make him understand that if she could only control the hunger.

It would be so easy to forget everything. Forget he near mortally wounded you. Forget he's the father of your child. Forget he's a married man. He certainly has. He expects you to lie back, invite him into your yearning body. Enjoy it.

Enjoy was a nothing word.

Once burned she was for ever marked.

The palm of his hand covered her breast. Her nipple was so painfully taut she gave an involuntary gasp as his palm brushed it. Her stomach muscles spasmed. What they were doing was scandalous.

She jerked away in a panic, pressing her hand hard against his chest. "No."

"No? Catrina, you crazy woman, you were loving it. We both want it." His tone was ragged with intimacy.

"I'm too full of pride." Her whole body was shuddering, trying to cope with the assault on her senses.

The past was as yesterday.

He felt driven beyond endurance. "Pride, really?" His hands shot out of their own accord, clenching her shoulders. "What does a treacherous woman like you have to do with pride?" His blue eyes flashed lightning.

She had to force herself to speak. That he could say that! "Go!" She was gripped by a helpless rage. "Go." Before the whole fragile edifice of her self-control collapsed in a cloud of dust.

She sounded as though he intended to harm her. "Just how sane are you?"

"I'm not sane at all." *Not around* you. *The love of my life. The enemy. How I hate you for it.*

There was a harsh mocking edge to his voice. "You're a remarkable woman, Catrina, but critical little bits and pieces have been left out of your genetic code," he said, preparing to leave.

"Not to the extent of yours," she shot back, his opponent. "Goodnight, Ashe, or should I say Lord

Wyndham? I remembered you're a married man even if you didn't."

Everything she was saying was hitting him blindside. Fancy *her* taking the high moral ground. He nearly told her then he had never married, only damn her! She was the one who had betrayed him yet she was acting the part of a victim. It didn't make sense. He could hear his mother's voice:

Julian, my darling, the poor girl needed help. Lots of help. She was just using you. Using us. She'll probably spend her time when she gets back home amusing her friends with what was no more to her than an adventure.

His mother had talked and talked until he was drained of all emotion. His mother had never thought his love for Catrina was a fairy story. His sisters had not been so severe, but they too had been shocked and confused.

I had thought you two were madly in love. That from Olivia, shaking her head. *You were the one, Ashe, who was building the dream. I'm so, so sorry.*

She wasn't cut out to be your wife, Julian darling, his mother had lamented. *Perhaps she was frightened of taking on a new way of life? Eighteen is just a baby after all.*

And that was the last he ever heard from her. A pretty destructive "baby".

Cate shut the door on him, promising herself...

promising herself...that would never happen again. The urge had been on them to make love, satisfy a physical hunger. That was all it was.

Shame for her own weakness hung over her.

CHAPTER SIX

ON THE FOLLOWING Monday afternoon he drove the car put at his disposal to the house where she lived. He parked in the leafy tree-lined street looking upwards. The house looked pretty impressive from the outside. Built on the side of a hill, it would have a stunning view of the blue marina he had passed along the way. Not that marinas weren't scattered all around the harbour. This was an island continent. People loved their boats. Loved their sailing. He knew the famous Sydney Hobart Yacht Race had become an icon of Australian sport attracting yachts from all around the world as well as a huge international media coverage. So there was sailing, swimming and of course the cricket.

He was a mite surprised at how beautiful Sydney was, how dynamic, very cosmopolitan. It was a world-class city with a harbour that was a splendid asset. Then there was the climate! Day after day of glorious sunshine, beautiful and balmy breezes off the harbour. Catrina had always made jokes about their English "never ending" rain but he had sometimes thought she secretly enjoyed it. Or a certain amount of it anyway. She had certainly enjoyed the snow. She had never seen snow in her entire life or the wonderland it created. So many times over the years he had kept coming back to their walks in the snow.

Fresh snow had fallen during the night. He had prayed for it. The months of October and November had been unusually warm, but in these days before Christmas the snow had set in. A Godsend! They badly wanted to be alone together. He was amazed at the strength of the bond that had grown so swiftly between them. It was as though they had known and loved one another in another life. Was that possible? Millions of people believed in reincarnation. What he did know was, she was everything...everything...he wanted in a woman: beautiful, glowing, clever, full of curiosity with such a broad range of interests. He knew she was ambitious. She had plans. He knew she was the sort of girl who would have and he approved of that. Only he needed to be a part of her plans. She already was with him. In the deepest caverns of his heart he knew she was the answer to his dream.

He helped her into her warm topcoat, then for

extra measure wound a cashmere scarf around her neck. She wore an emerald cap on her head that accentuated the colour of her eyes. He had found a soft pair of gloves for her hands. They were ridiculously big.

"You love looking after me, don't you?" She looked up at him, flipping her thick blonde braid over the collar.

"I want to look after you all our lives." There didn't seem to be any other kind of answer.

"Terrific!" At eighteen she might have been fearful of such an early declaration. No, she embraced it, holding up her face for his kiss. Her face was so radiant he thought he had never seen anything so glorious in his life. "You'll make a wonderful husband, a wonderful father," she told him as soon as her mouth was free. They were too close to the house. They found it restricting with so many eyes on them.

"That shows what an excellent judge of character you are," he joked. Their emotions were so deep, so overwhelming, their falling so passionately in love had transformed their lives. They hadn't had sex. They had come close. But not yet. It was enough for now for the two of them to be together. He knew he was going to make love to her the way he wanted. He knew he wouldn't be able to help it. All her responses incited him. He knew her flame of desire would fire up to meet his.

Snowflakes fell through the chilly air, landing on their heads and shoulders.

"Angel dust strewn from the heavens," she cried, lifting her lovely face. "God's gift to the world."

"The grounds look even better in midwinter," he told her. "The contrast between dark and snow-white is surreal."

"Like stepping into a dream." She was laughing, hugging him like this was such an adventure. She talked about the way Turner had painted the most sublime and romantic Alpine snowscapes. She told him it had actually snowed in Bethlehem the Christmas before. She told him she could roller skate. She was sure she could perform as well on ice. There was so much they wanted to do together. They had plenty of time. He would make sure of that, although he had to return to Oxford to complete a joint honours degree in Law and Economics. The family retained an apartment in London. He would find somewhere else. Somewhere suitable for just him and Catrina.

To doubt they would always be together was to doubt that destiny had brought them to this moment in time.

At least he had been destined not to die before seeing her again, he thought grimly. Such were the glories and tribulations of life. Breakdowns

in relationships brought a lot of stress into lives.
People *did* die, some chose to die, of a broken
heart. He had responsibilities and his own brand
of pride. What he felt now was a deepening need
to address the events of the past. So much of it
didn't make sense. Or was he only seeing clearly
now. As he sat there staring up at the house where
she lived memories began tugging at him again.
They were so poignant they caught at his heart.
She had snared him that very first day; ended by
sabotaging his life.

*"How many acres to the estate?" she asked, look-
ing around her. The sheen of excitement, almost
rapture, had brought a flush of colour to her
cheeks.*

*It was a lovely face, perfectly symmetrical, the
eyes a crystalline green, the creamy skin flawless, the mouth with a luscious fullness. She really
was a beautiful woman. "Approx two hundred,"
he said, pretending offhandedness when he was
amazed to find things were actually getting pretty
heavy. For that matter he had felt a bolt of pleasure the instant his eyes had fallen on her spir-
ited, challenging face. Now she was staring up at
the hall as if at a vision, something from a fairy
tale. One would have thought she'd travelled halfway around the world just to see it. He couldn't*

quite grasp the extent of her interest. It seemed a shade extreme.

"How splendid!" she breathed. "Go on, how many rooms?" She had looked to him for the answer.

He obliged. "The reception hall, four reception rooms, I'm not sure how many bedrooms, certainly a dozen. Quite a few bathrooms. No en suites. Housekeeper's accommodation, stables, coach house, tennis court. There's a lake with white swans, a stone bridge over it. Thinking of buying it, are you?" he asked very blandly. It was a defence mechanism. A lot of emotions were stirring in him. He had to slap them down fast. She was reeling him in much too easily for his liking. They'd only just met!

"How do you know I'm not an heiress?" she retorted, sounding amused.

He gave her another appraising glance. She looked back. They went on looking at each other. For much too long. He would have to take care not to run off the road. Or he could sneak glances at her when she was looking the other way. "Heiresses usually travel in their own private limousines," he said crisply.

"Easier to travel incognito," she replied airily. "Do we take the main driveway to the house or do we have to go around the back, the tradesmen entrance?"

"Why not make it an exhilarating experience for you?" he suggested. *"How come the English accent, by the way? That's a bit of a puzzle unless your parents are English and migrated."*

"For a better life," she said shortly.

For a moment he had thought she was on the verge of saying more but stifled it. *"Or they never worked a day in their lives? That's an English public-school accent with a trace of Oz thrown in."*

She weighed up what he said with a frown. *"You obviously have remarkable powers of deduction."*

"Too close for comfort maybe?" he shot off.

"Don't be absurd." There was an edge to her voice. She tossed back her golden head. *"My... mother is English."*

It was clear she wasn't going to say anything more.

Woman of mystery. She looked exactly the part. It was a great pity his best girl, Marina, didn't look or act a bit more like her. He shouldn't really be comparing the two. Marina certainly didn't lack a very attractive appearance. She was a good friend—he had known her from childhood—a lovely person, but she didn't have what Catrina had. More was the pity. Marina was an earl's daughter, but extraordinarily enough she lacked the cool arrogance of this Australian beauty. Neither did Marina have the sweeping confidence in herself. Their positions could have been reversed.

It suddenly struck him it was possible to become obsessed by a woman. He had never understood it before. He'd never had a lot of sympathy for men who allowed it to happen. Now a young goddess with exceptional powers had crossed his path. He was already wondering what it would be like to kiss her. He knew, somehow, he would. He definitely didn't want her to disappear.

Which was exactly what she did. How wicked was that?

He was just about to restart the car, when a silver car looking slightly the worse for wear pulled up at the foot of the incline. A moment later a good-looking, stylishly dressed woman in her late forties-early fifties stepped gracefully out of the back seat followed by a boy around seven, wearing a school uniform. He was a very handsome boy with a shock of thick blond hair that shone in the sun. He was dragging what looked like a too-heavy schoolbag behind him. Another boy seated in the passenger seat wound down his window to throw his friend his school hat.

"See you tomorrow, Jules," he called breezily. "Goodbye, Mrs Hamilton." This time the tone was very respectful.

For a moment he felt his brain seize up. *Jules? Mrs Hamilton?* "God, oh, God," he muttered. "No, it can't be." There was a roaring in his ears; pain in his body as though a car had collected him, throwing him against a brick wall. He was having what was loosely termed an *epiphany*.

Jules? His friend Bill Gascoyne often called him Jules, rather than the preferred Ashe. But he couldn't possibly consider what was before him. Not for a moment. Yet he found himself straining to see the faces of the woman and the boy as they started up the incline. How he needed his binoculars! The driver of the car who had decided against driving up the slope took off with a wave. He knew exactly where the pair was going. To the elegant sandstone house with the delicately ornate cast-iron lace balustrades, decorative posts and valances.

Catrina's home.

The slim, dark-haired woman had to be her mother. The boy was Catrina's son. She had said he was five. A lie. His sister Olivia and her husband, Bram, had a six-year-old boy, Peter. This boy was taller and more developed. He had to be going on seven. He couldn't shake a profoundly disturbing thought. Was it possible this fair-headed boy was his own son? The thought nearly made his head cave in. Even Catrina wouldn't have done such a cruel, cruel thing. His eyes still hadn't left the pair, woman and boy. The boy had his head uplifted, talking in an animated fashion to his grandmother. Probably giving her the news of the day.

Clearly they were devoted to each other. There was something about the woman that suggested perhaps he had met her before? Not possible. Yet he felt a very strong reaction inside.

He sat there a little longer. What to do? He was more shaken than he could have imagined. Even the first sight of Catrina hadn't done this. He knew he was never going to get an invitation to the house. He had to act. Put an end to this. Catrina wouldn't be home for some hours yet. He would go to the house, introduce himself. He needed to see the boy's face. For that matter he needed to see the woman's face. She reminded him of someone. He didn't know who. He could come up with some excuse for calling in on them. A courtesy call to all appearances when inside he was ferociously intent. Had he known it, his blue eyes were blazing. The boy had obviously inherited Catrina's glorious blonde hair. He wanted to believe the boy's eyes would be a crystalline green or even dark. The woman had dark hair. He had a clear sense her eyes would be dark as well.

He got out of the car, locked it with the button on his key. His expression was grim. He was intent on the task ahead. It could be a big mistake he was making. On the other hand it could prove to be a mind-blowing revelation.

He crossed the road, struggling for control.

The woman opened the door, a look of enquiry

on her face. "Can I help you?" As she looked up at the tall, arrestingly handsome man at her door her expression splintered and her body began to shake slightly.

Stella's brain had turned to mush. She lost all track of time. Here before her in the flesh was a Carlisle. No doubting it. The Carlisle sapphire-blue, thickly lashed eyes. The height, the military-type bearing, the outstanding good looks. She remembered his late father, Geoffrey, had that thin aristocratic nose, the fine carriage, the set of the shoulders. An Englishman. Geoffrey had married that dreadful girl, Alicia Scott-Lennox, who had thought herself more royal than royalty itself. God knew why! She had hidden her worst side from Geoffrey. One had to wonder for how long?

"I think you can," the stranger who was never a stranger responded, unable to keep the shock and outrage out of his tone. Wyndham was stunned to see that the woman before him, the woman who had disappeared from all family life for more than a quarter century, was Stella Radclyffe. It was her sister, Annabel, who had remained. Annabel, the flighty one, the acknowledged beauty who had married a man old enough to be her father. Money, of course.

Well, the game was over now.

"You know who I am?" The tension in his tall,

lean body revealed the extent of his shock. Indeed shock radiated off him.

Stella, too, was making a tremendous effort to pull herself together. "You're Lord Wyndham, of course," she said, with open hostility. "You became my father's heir." Here was the man who had not only broken Cate's heart, but had now returned to disrupt their happy lives.

"Which makes you a kinswoman of mine, Stella Radclyffe that was." It was a statement, not a question, delivered with what she considered magnificent arrogance.

"I suppose there's no point in denying it." Stella threw back her head.

"No point at all," he agreed. "May I come in?" Behind her he could see into the spacious hallway, elegantly furnished with a curving staircase beyond it.

"I'm sorry." Stella stood firm, holding on to her not-inconsiderable nerve. "Cate should be here. She won't be home until well after six. Why do you want to see her anyway? You've done nothing but harm." Her breath rasped in her throat.

Harm? That gave him a jolt. He decided not to pursue it. "I'd like to see the boy," he replied. "Don't be afraid I will say anything to him. I just want to *see* him."

Stella's face had turned bone-white, but her tone

was tightly controlled. "Not possible. My grandson has nothing whatever to do with you."

"Spare me," he groaned, having trouble processing what the hell was going on with this woman. "Why are you so frightened? What could you possibly have to hide? You and Catrina." His blue eyes slashed.

Stella's tongue, for once, was unguarded. "Aren't you the man who betrayed her?" she challenged. She was going out on the attack, feeling near hysterical under an avalanche of deep resentments.

"For goodness' sake!" He didn't deign to respond, the expression on his striking face openly contemptuous. "Allow me to see the boy and I'll go away. I give you my word."

He didn't need to add: *But I'll be back.*

Stella held up a hand. "I'm sorry."

"Are you?" he asked simply. "What did Catrina tell you about me—a pack of lies?"

"You're married, aren't you? You have children?"

Tell her.

He was about to when a child's voice called loudly and, it had to be said, belligerently from somewhere at the top of the stairs. "I'm here, Nan." The tone signalled the boy was ready to defend his nan and the house if need be.

"Do not upset him," Stella was reduced to begging.

"As if I would," he said shortly, maddened by

her attitude. The next moment a boy who had to be around seven years old raced down the stairs, his expression growing more protective the closer he came to the front door. "Who are *you*?" He looked up at Wyndham, taking his grandmother's trembling hand. "Why are you standing there? What do you want?"

Wyndham's heart bounced, but remarkably his reply was both calm and quelling. "I was simply paying my respects to your grandmother. She happens to be a kinswoman of mine."

So why the strained faces? Jules pondered. "I don't believe you," he said flatly, though he was fairly certain the man was telling the truth.

"I could provide you with proof. I'm Julian Carlisle, by the way, and you're Jules, Catrina's son." Wyndham held out his hand.

It was such an authoritative hand, Jules was compelled to take it. This man *had* to be okay. He looked important.

"It's a great pleasure to meet you, Jules." Wyndham shook his son's hand, looking down into the Carlisles' vivid blue eyes. No mistaking them. Though the boy had Catrina's blond hair as he grew he would display more and more Carlisle physical characteristics. The height. The chiselled features. Right now he was just a beautiful, brave little boy coming swiftly to his grandmother's defence. Anyone would admire that. Wyndham did.

"How come my first name is the same as yours?" Jules asked, staring up at the man, his brain seeking answers.

Stella put a protective hand on his shoulder. "Jules," she hushed.

"Well, it's not such an uncommon name, is it?" Wyndham suggested and smiled.

That smile directed right at him made Jules' breath catch somewhere in his chest. He didn't know why except it was a *great* smile. People always told him he had a great smile. It struck him that despite the funny atmosphere he *liked* this man. He looked one hundred per cent trustworthy. Anyone would be proud to have him for a... for a...dad.

Jules turned his head to stare up at his grandmother, saw the worry on her face. "What's wrong, Nan?" he asked. Why wasn't Nan inviting their visitor in? She was normally softly spoken, but he had heard Nan speaking with frost bite in her tone. Was she really a relative of his? Then it hit Jules. The voices. Same kind of posh accent. Nan was English. His gaze flashed back to the man. The man was too. "You're Lord Wyndham, aren't you?" he asked as a door in his mind opened.

Wyndham could only nod. He felt like a man who had been robbed of what he would have held most precious.

His son.

His son denied him for long, empty years. He had thought of it as the abyss. What Catrina had done was diabolical. All right she had cut him out of her life. She had no right to cut out his child. He wanted to do something drastic. He wanted to rant and rage as he had never done. He had locked it all in. He wanted Catrina right there before him. Preferably on her knees, her slender neck bent, ready for the sword. He wanted the *truth*. He felt capable of forcing it out of her. But when he spoke it was with an air of apology. "My fault, Jules, I'm afraid. I gave your grandmother a shock. I should have rung ahead, but I wanted to surprise her."

Jules began to nod his understanding, then broke off as further uncertainties set in. "There's something I don't understand," he said.

It was issued like a real challenge, Wyndham thought. The boy was displaying his intelligence and his finely tuned perceptions, exceptional for one so young.

"No matter, Jules." Wyndham began to turn away. "Your mother will explain it to you."

"Explain what? Wouldn't it be better if you did?" Jules started to follow the man as he walked down the short flight of stone steps.

Wyndham turned. "No, your mother will do it. Go back inside, Jules," he said with quiet but unmistakeable authority. He lifted a hand to Stella, who was standing like a pillar of salt. "I'll phone Catrina when I get back to the hotel," he said.

My God, I have to warn her, Stella thought.

"Goodbye now, Jules," he called.

"Goodbye, sir." The man's smile washed over Jules again. It was like sunlight. It restored Jules' sense of comfort and well-being.

"Will I see you again?" he called with a betraying eagerness in his voice. This was a real live lord. Wait until he told Noah! Not that either of them would want to be one. They were *Australian*.

Wyndham raised a hand. "Sure to, Jules," he said.

Try explaining this away, Catrina. Try it, just try it.

The words reeled away like a mantra in his head.

Once Stella shut the door, Jules wouldn't leave it alone. "You're his kinswoman. That's a relative, isn't it, Nan?"

Jules was into discovery. Next he'd be onto Ancestry.com. "Yes, darling," Stella said, desperate to get to the phone. "The funny thing is I never laid eyes on him until today."

"Why's that?" Jules grabbed at her hand. "Why have you never gone back to England for a visit? Aunty Annabel used to visit you, didn't she? I think I remember her."

"You probably do, although you were only five."

"What happened to her?" Jules asked.

"Aunt Annabel died young, dear, because she never looked after herself. She mixed with the wrong people."

"That's sad. I hope her dying was peaceful?" Jules said from the depths of his tender heart.

"Very peaceful, darling," Stella assured him. "Now, what would you like for afternoon tea? Something light. I have roast chicken and all the trimmings for dinner."

Jules gave her the strangest look. "Don't you want to talk about it, Nan?"

She paused to look down at him. "What's *it*, darling?"

"I was listening from the top of the stairs. You sounded like you were a bit afraid of him. Were you?"

"Certainly not!" Stella pronounced firmly. "I suppose I was a bit overwhelmed. He is a lord, you know. The fifth Baron Wyndham."

"Aunt Annabel was a lady. Does that mean you were one too before you came to Australia? We don't have lords and ladies here, thank goodness. I think we should all be the same."

Stella's smile was grim. "You could be right. I was a very modest Miss Stella Radclyffe, as was Annabel." In fact both had had the title of The Honourable, but she didn't bother telling him that.

"My sister, Annabel, married a hugely successful businessman, Sir Nigel Warren, who was knighted by the Queen. Therefore she had the title Lady Warren."

"I see. But it is better when everyone is the same," Jules pronounced, "yet part of me was impressed. I thought Lord Wyndham was really cool. He looks a bit like some painting I've seen in a book. Sort of haughty, but I think, kind. I can't wait for Mummy to get home. Should you ring her and tell her?"

Stella almost sighed aloud in relief. "What a good idea. You go upstairs and get changed and I'll ring your mother."

And that was what Stella did.

Catrina listened in silence, then said, "God help us all! He knows, doesn't he?"

"Of course he knows," Stella said with a severity that was palpable even over the phone. "I'd abandon any attempt to pull the wool over his eyes."

"Isn't it *eyes* what this is all about? Living proof," Cate said, halfway between gravity and black humour.

"Is it ever!" Stella rasped. "Jules liked him," she said, as though that were a betrayal.

"Of course he did!" Cate responded. "What's the big surprise? They're blood. I have to go, Stella. Thanks for warning me. Ashe won't let this lie. I kept the existence of his son from him for seven years. I suppose he had the right to know," she admitted unexpectedly.

"You remember what he did to you," Stella reminded her with some wrath. "Just don't panic. Be strong."

"You're the strong one, Stell."

"I'm not." Well, she *was*, but in all modesty it was her habit to dismiss it.

"You certainly are when it comes to pulling your weight. I want you to know I think you do a great job with Jules." Catrina put down the phone. The sky outside her floor-to-ceiling office window was a deep blue.

But a storm was coming.

Murphy Stiller, wearing another one of her power suits, barged into her office without knocking. "Finished the Mangan proposal yet?" Her ill humour was evident.

"Not only finished, I've run it all by Hugh," Cate said blithely. "Anything else I can help you with, Murphy?"

No reply. The usual glare.

"I mean, it's not as though we're buddies." A note of derision had entered her voice.

"Hardly." Murphy gave her a smile of sheer malevolence. "I don't care much for you."

"Not a lot of people care for you, Murphy," Cate

pointed out. "Probably not even your mother." Cate once had been drawn into a long, informative chat with Murphy's large and formidable mother.

"Let's keep my mother out of this." Murphy bit down hard on her lip. "My mother is a tyrant. She's also a desperately unhappy woman."

"If so, I'm sorry to hear it." Mrs Stiller, like her daughter, Murphy, was a born bully with the devil in her. Blood would out.

"Well, I couldn't care less," Murphy cried, unrepentant. "She dotes on my brother, Alex, but she thinks I've never measured up."

Instantly Cate felt pity. Fancy growing up with Mrs Stiller for a mother. "I'm sure she doesn't. You're a highly successful woman."

Murphy didn't thank her for the comment. "So how did you and Lord Wyndham get along?" Her near-black eyes were full of innuendo. "Kept him happy, did you?"

"Get your head into gear," Cate said shortly. "How come you felt it necessary to tell him I had a son?"

Murphy had the grace to flush. "Tell you, did he?"

Cate kept her expression neutral. "It was of little interest to him, but I'm getting a bit tired of your interference in my private affairs, Murphy. You've done it many times. The next time I'll go to Hugh."

"And complain?" Murphy's loud challenge would have blown another woman to smithereens.

"You bet," Cate said. "I know you love your job, Murphy. Think about it."

Murphy Stiller's olive cheeks took on a hot flush. "Think you could get me fired? So poor old Hugh has the hots for you, does that make you think you're invincible?"

"Is anybody?" Cate asked. "I'm sick of these references to Hugh's attraction to me. Hugh is a hundred per cent loyal to his wife. So lay off, Murphy. Now I don't have time to talk, so you'll have to excuse me. Would you mind shutting the door when you go?"

Murphy did her stuff. She gave the door one almighty slam.

Thirty minutes later Cate was trying hard to focus on a mining lease, when the phone rang.

She knew who it was before she lifted the phone. "Wyndham."

"What can I do for you, Wyndham?" She spoke with cool detachment. She could have been a great actress. No trouble at all. "Is something wrong?"

"Now I know the reason why you've been so worried." His tone was so much like a whiplash it brought the blood to her skin. "Make any excuse you like, but I expect to see you at my hotel in under a half hour."

"Impossible," she said. "I've work to do."

The steely tone was calculated to get anyone moving. "Thirty minutes," he said. "Don't show up, I'm coming after you. I can promise you it won't be pleasant. Far better we have our conversation here."

It reminded Cate of the many TV crime shows she had watched, where a suspect was offered the option of spilling the beans right where they stood, or going down to the police station.

She let the phone fall. She had to head off for his hotel.

CHAPTER SEVEN

HE LET HER IN. Fury was burning like a slow fuse. When it hit the target it would burst into a conflagration.

His target was her. Yet she threw her arms extravagantly into the air as if she didn't have a care in the world

It was the signal for him to turn on her, his body so taut Cate was made fully aware of the power in him. "I've never known anyone like you," he said, in a hard, unforgiving voice.

"So you used to say." Her comment was foolishly facetious, adding fuel to the fire.

"Don't make me angrier than I already am," he warned. "Your mother rang you, of course?"

"My adopted mother," Cate found herself saying, taking an armchair. "She's a jolly old Radclyffe, you know. You're related."

"That jolly old Radclyffe who just happened to have been born at Radclyffe Hall washed her hands of her own family. She's your *real* mother, your biological mother. She had to have a reason for running off to Australia. Pregnant no doubt, which doesn't make sense as she was a married woman."

"Stella had her reasons. She *did* adopt me. I have the papers."

He stared at her as though convinced she was a pathological liar. "I don't believe you."

Her own temper flared. "Harsh words aren't they? Especially coming from someone like you."

"Is that the best you can do?" he exclaimed, dropping into the chair opposite her. Even then his eyes were involuntarily drinking her in, he thought in disgust. "Your boy, Jules, is my son."

"What if I swear he isn't?"

"You could swear like the worst inmate in your worst jail. Jules is my son. You were pregnant when you left England."

"I wasn't."

He ignored that, his eyes ablaze.

"Okay, I was," she admitted. It would be too easy for him to prove paternity. That was if he wanted to. Her only hope was he would simply go away. "I wasn't really sure until a couple of months later. I should tell you it came as a huge shock. When the doctor told me I screamed so loud it's a wonder you didn't hear me deep in the Cotswolds."

He bent forward as though he couldn't bear to

look at her. "This is it, is it?" he asked with contempt. "You're going to confront the gravest matter with your silly jokes."

"No joke, I assure you," she said so sharply he lifted his dark head. "Giving birth is no fun."

"God, Catrina," he breathed. "Have you even for a moment regretted not letting me know? I have rights. Have you forgotten about that, about common decency? I would have done everything in my power to help you."

She lit up with anger. "*How* exactly? Have money put into my bank account?"

His black brows knitted. "I would have come on the first plane."

She turned her head away. "That's as big a lie as it gets. You cut me out of your life, Ashe. You and your horrible mother."

That got to him. Horrible mother? He felt like shaking her. "What does my mother have to answer for?" he rasped. "She was as shocked as I was by your defection. She stood by me. I couldn't have asked for stronger support."

Cate, too, was nearly jumping out of her skin. "Your mother was a *monster*," she cried.

He looked utterly shocked, so shocked she floundered. "She *was*." She registered she had lost it.

"My mother is dead," he said. His expression

was fixed yet incredibly alert like a big cat about to pounce.

"What?" she gasped.

"Hard of hearing, are you? My mother is dead. She was very badly injured in a riding accident. She died a few days later in hospital."

Cate felt her skin blanch. "What can I say? I'm sorry? I *am* sorry, but your mother was hateful to me."

He gave an incredulous laugh. "Catrina, I'm finding this very hard to believe. If my mother was hateful to you I can only say she hid it extremely well."

"From *you*," Cate retorted. "I grant you she was pleasant enough right up until our last confrontation. Then she made it abundantly clear where she really stood. She told me it was time for me to get myself back off to Australia. Disappear from your life. I simply wasn't good enough. Marina only just made it. Perhaps she'd been aiming for one of the royal princesses?"

He felt as if his head were spinning. "What in the name of God are you talking about? You expect me to believe my own mother behaved in that way?"

"I don't care what you believe," she said flatly.

He lurched to his feet. "Catrina, try to see this my way, I beg you. Apart from anything else, my mother isn't around to refute these charges. All *I* know is, she was so upset she could barely show me your *pathetic* note."

An icy sensation enveloped Cate. "How could she show you a note when I never *left* one?" she shouted. "Why would I, for God's sake? Like a coward—I never thought you were that—you scuttled off to London while your mother did your dirty work."

"Hey, hey, hey," he warned. "Go no further."

He looked furious, even disoriented, his eyes a stunning flame-blue. She decided it was time to beat a retreat, even though she knew he would never lay a hand on her.

"Don't you *dare* leave." His voice was a deep, dark purr low in his chest.

She took a panicky breath. "You can't touch me. I'll have you up on a charge." She made the empty threat.

"You'll have us *both* up," he said. "Come back and sit down, Catrina. I don't assault women, even women without a conscience, like you. What I'd really like to know is, how can such a lovely creature be so downright cruel?"

Her legs were so unsteady beneath her she had to resume her seat. "You were the one who screwed me up, Ashe. I loved you with all my heart."

He towered over her. "I won't listen to you."

"You listened to your mother. Don't you want to hear what *I* have to say?"

"Not right now," he said very tightly. "I don't think I could handle it. I just want you to admit one thing. Your child is my son."

"Hell with it!" she cried. "Yes, yes, *yes*!"

"That's all I need to know. My son, my precious, *precious* son!"

It was coming…it was coming…the Storm. Important she be ready. No one on earth would take Jules from her. "So what do you intend to do about it?" She threw out the challenge. "Have him over to England for the holidays? Let him mix with your kids?"

His eyes flashed lightning. "What makes you think I have kids?"

"Well, don't you?" She leapt to her feet again, unable to sit still. "Or is Marina barren? It can't be *you*. You got me pregnant in no time at all."

"You can never fix this, Cate," he said.

The first time he had ever used the shortened version of her name. It shook her badly. "That's irrelevant now. I want you to stay away from me, Ashe. Stay away from my son. I'll tell him about you in time. Not yet. Not until he's old enough to understand. I'd like to leave now."

"That's what you do, though, isn't it—*run*? What you can't deal with, you run from. Were you nervous about my taking up the peerage? What it might entail for you?"

She gave a laugh that was more than a little on the wild side. "Don't be so stupid."

"What was it, then?" he demanded. "Tell me. Tell me the truth and I'll let you go."

She was horrendously upset but she had to fight. Only how could she continue to attack his mother? Mothers were sacred. Sons always defended their mothers. That was the way of it. She knew how protective seven-year-old Jules was of her. "I did tell you, Ashe, but you wouldn't believe me," she said with more restraint. "I know your mother adored you. I know how much you loved her, your sisters, your family. You were the perfect son. She had lost her husband. She had to hold on to her son. To do that, she had to rule your life. Your mother didn't have a real problem with me until it became known you were heir to the baronetcy. She thought I was just a summer flirtation, a fling. Soon enough I would go back home. End of story. End of concern. You would marry Marina and live happily ever after."

"Except I didn't marry Marina," he exclaimed, trying to cope with what she was saying.

"What?" Her voice rose steeply despite her determination to keep calm. She stared at him with stunned eyes.

His tone was soft and deadly. "I didn't marry

Marina. She married one of my closest friends. You met him. Simon Bolton."

Simon, of course. She shook her head, not able to conceal her amazement. "But she was deeply in love with you. I wasn't such a fool I didn't know that."

"Sadly I wasn't in love with her," he said with more than a trace of regret. "I was in love with some sort of a…" he hesitated, searching for the right word "…sociopath."

"To whom you were deeply attracted," she pointed out furiously. "Don't worry, there are a lot of sociopaths about," she said. "Mostly men. Women marry charming, generous, caring men only to find out a short time later their dark, abusive side. Only the other day, before the happy couple got to the wedding reception he bashed her up. You see, we're never really sure who we're dealing with. I learned that lesson fairly early in life. So who did you eventually marry? Hang on!" She held up a hand. "I think I know. It was Marina's friend, the dark-haired one with the lovely glowing skin and the unusual name…Talisa?"

He didn't answer, as though he didn't have to acknowledge it. Yet he had been prepared to be unfaithful to Talisa only nights ago, Cate thought.

"Think Talisa can handle your love child? It could come as a shock too difficult to bear."

His silence continued as though he were groping

through a minefield to find answers. "I have your last note to me," he said finally. "Let me show it to you." His suit jacket was hanging over a chair. She saw his expensive crocodile-skin wallet lying on the table. He picked it up, extracting a folded, rather tattered-looking piece of paper.

"This is my note?" she asked in sharp derision. "I can't wait to read it."

Note, what note?

Much of life was a mystery.

"So how is my son doing at school?" he enquired as he passed the sheet of yellowing paper to her.

Cate frowned, gingerly beginning to open the sheet of paper up. "He's doing fine. He's clever. Like me."

"Or he's even cleverer. Like *me*."

Cate nodded impatiently, intent on absorbing the contents. They were handwritten in her rather distinctive script. To her horror, it looked like her handwriting only it *wasn't*. There was something terribly wrong here. She really needed a forensic tool to make a detailed inspection. Were there tiny breaks in the flowing script as if someone had rested a second before going on? She never did that. Her writing was continuous without break. Finally she made her decision, though she knew it would meet with extreme hostility. She looked directly at him. "Anybody, absolutely *anybody*, could have written this."

"*You're* the one," he returned trenchantly. "I compared it with all the little love notes you used to leave for me. 'How do I love thee? Let me count the ways.'"

"More like how do I *hate* thee."

"It's *your* handwriting, fine handwriting really with a few little eccentricities. The embellished C of Catrina, for instance. It's there."

"Of course it is. Essential to do it like that. Only you have to prove *I* was the one to do it. It might look like my handwriting but I didn't write this. Not in a million light years." Then it dawned on her. She spoke up knowing he would hate her. "Your mother wrote this," she said, not with a note of shock but comprehension. "I'm sure of it."

His mother? He suddenly felt a lack of oxygen, rallied fast. "Drop the tone and the accusation," he warned.

"Don't try intimidating me, Ashe," she said, angling her delicately determined chin. "Don't even think of it. I'm not the naïvely trusting girl I once was. You take a little moment to think about it. Your mother was a talented artist. I saw countless sketch books of her drawings over the years. Numerous sketches of you in particular, her darling only son. Your sisters were well back in the queue. They had to accept one of the realities of life. Mothers fixate on sons. Then there were Alicia's watercolours. She was gifted." Jules had followed in her footsteps; Cate had long since accepted that. Such was the permanence of *blood*. Jules had inherited Alicia's talent. His recent sketches of her and Stella were very good, even capturing their expressions. Jules had taken them to school and the art teacher had praised him, posting them up.

For a moment she felt real sadness, as though Alicia's presence was hovering over them. She covered up her angst by looking down again at the letter. It read:

Dearest Ashe,
Don't hate me but I can't bear to stay. You're lovely but I had no idea what I was getting myself into. I don't want your life. It scares me. The voice inside me is telling me to go home. You and I would never work. Not for long. You have Marina. She'll suit you far better than me. I'm not feeling good about it—I know we had started to make plans— but I realise now I'm not ready for any of it. I'm too young. The more I've thought it through, the surer I am I'm doing the right thing. By the time you read this I'll be back home where I belong. We had great times, but they're over. Please don't try to contact me. That's the last thing I want. Have a good life.
Catrina.

Cate had to shut her eyes on the misery she had endured. The thoughts of betrayal she had battled so long might not have been so. Alicia had simply taken matters into her own autocratic hands.

"Not exactly an epic," she said, not letting her pain surface. "How many words—one hundred or so? Your mother, sadly, was a woman not to be trusted where you were concerned. She loved you. You loved her. It's terrible for me to have to speak about her with so much disrespect, but your mother wrote this. Not me." She fluttered the sheet of paper in the air. "Put it back in your wallet. Why have you carried it all these years anyway?"

"To remind me," he said with great abruptness.

"I would have thought you'd destroy it."

He was staring at her as though he was trying to look into her bruised and battered soul. Did he believe her? Mothers were sacrosanct.

Only Alicia had changed everything. She might be floating around somewhere but she no longer had her earthly force. "Get some forensic people onto it," Cate suggested. "It's not my writing, although at a cursory glance even I thought it was." His mother would have made a first-rate forger.

He was an expert in concealing his emotions, but there was something frightening in the intensity of his expression, the blaze in his eyes. "I cannot believe my own mother would have done anything to hurt me," he said with a twist to his mouth. "And so badly. I mean, she *saw* my pain, for God's sake. I loved and respected her even if I knew she was a mite possessive. But that was her nature." He continued to stare at Catrina, seeing a beautiful young woman with her golden hair and her crystal-clear green eyes with an unnatural clarity. How could such beauty hide so much darkness and deception? It didn't seem possible. He had to confront the possibility Catrina might well have been as much a victim as he was.

"Your mother built up a great case against me, Ashe," she said quietly, seeing his perceptions of his mother were badly shaken. "I'm equally sure she thought she was doing the right thing, protecting you from me. She thought I was the wrong person to become part of your life. You were to become the fifth Baron Wyndham. I didn't pass muster. You needed a *Somebody* at your side. That's the way you lot are. You needed an earl's daughter. You already had her—Marina. Marina was not part of this. Not part of your mother's manoeuvring. It was your mother who deliberately drove me away."

His handsome face bore such a torn expression. "Forget my poor mother for a moment. I can't handle it right now. You talk about deliberation? Then consider, if you will, you deliberately withheld from me the fact I had a son. You robbed me of my child for over seven years. You robbed me of so many great joys. I missed all of those early years, years that can never be retrieved. Justice must be served. I want my son back. Not only want, I *will* get him back, if I have to pursue you through the courts."

"It's not an easy task to separate a child from its mother, Ashe."

"I'll do it." He had to find a solution.

"You *can't*!"

A chink in the armour. "Watch me."

Her inner voice kicked in. *You can't offer him money to go away.* Some men would take it if the amount were big enough. But he wasn't one of them. For one thing he was rich. Far richer than she could ever be.

"Why would I expect you to show any loyalty to me?" Cate's voice was unnaturally calm. She looked up at him without anger, but a tremendous backwash of grief. "All your loyalty is and always has been to your mother. Believe her versions of events, Ashe. It suits you to do that. *I* know what happened. I remember all too clearly. The pain has never gone away. I never did have a chance. And don't try telling me you didn't know your mother was a fearful snob. Your sisters openly admitted that. They made a joke of it. And your Number One position in her life, her adored only son. Sons guaranteed the family name. Sons inherited. Ask them. They'll remember. If it's a question of a battle I know you're the one with the big guns, but I'll fight you to the death. Jules is mine. I raised him alone. My advice to you is to go home. No need to tell your family. They don't need to know. There's no reason whatever to bring scandal down on the illustrious family name." Now there was bitterness in her tone.

His eyes burned over her. "Much of public life is scandal, Catrina," he reminded her. "You'll be hearing from me."

"Go for it. But if you have samples of my hand-writing, I'd advise you to take them to a hand-writing expert. Let them check the capital C in particular. That's the flag. Your mother was clever, but not clever enough. She must have had a job carrying all that guilt around."

For a moment he couldn't speak. Singularly disturbing thoughts were whirring about in his head. "And what if this expert confirms it *is* your hand-writing?"

"They won't," she said with utter conviction.

His expression had taken on a very determined cast. Indeed, everything about him was wound up so tight she went to the door.

"If they do confirm it's your handwriting, I'll destroy you," he warned, tremendously upset.

She laughed, totally without humour. "Except you destroyed me years ago."

That was her parting shot. Cate opened the door, allowing it to close after her.

She felt ill. What was it about mothers they could get away with just about anything? Alicia's efforts at forgery had been near perfect. She knew she wasn't the only woman whose romantic hopes had been dashed by the intervention of an overly possessive mother.

Only at long last Alicia was about to be found out.

That was if Ashe could bring himself to have her theory checked out. If he did, one problem would be solved. A far greater one remained. He had seen his beautiful son. He wanted him. He wanted to fit Jules into his family. Obviously he didn't think he would have a problem with Talisa. Why would he? She would adore him. Given a little time Talisa would settle.

Cate made the decision to see a solicitor right away.

No one would take her son from her. That wasn't about to happen. She wasn't frightened of a battle. She was up for it.

She faced the family solicitor of recent years, Gerald Enright, senior partner of the law firm Enright Matheson, across the expanse of his impressive partner's desk. Without an appointment Gerald had very kindly fitted her into his busy schedule,

but she only had thirty minutes. Grateful, she had
come prepared. She had it all in her head. A few
pleasantries, enquiries after Stella, a great favourite, then Gerald listened in silence before sum-
ming up.

"I have to tell you I'm astonished by all this,
Cate," he said. "Astonished matters have gone as
far as they have. Either one of you could have got
in touch with the other. So he's English and living
there. That doesn't constitute a problem. Distance
is no tyranny like in the old days."

She hadn't told him Ashe was the fifth Baron
Wyndham and a recent client of Inter-Austral. She
had referred to him only as Julian Carlisle.

"There is no doubt he is the father?" Gerald
asked in his courtly voice. Gerald was a handsome man nearing sixty. He had a full head of
silver hair, good unlined skin and piercing dark
eyes. His grey suit and blue and silver silk tie were
immaculate.

Cate shook her head. "None at all. To make matters worse, they share the same distinctive blue
eyes. Electric-blue. Frankly it's incredible. My son
has my blond colouring but he has Julian's eyes."

Gravely Gerald nodded. "Surely you don't expect him to go away, Cate? The fact you never told
him he had a son casts a different light on matters.
Clearly had he known he would have taken steps
to gain custody of his child."

"I raised my son alone, Gerald. I'm not giving him up," Cate said, trying to control her emotions. Jules was her Achilles heel.

"You may *have* to share custody, my dear," Gerald pointed out. "So try to prepare yourself. You say he has the money to fight you?"

"He's a wealthy man," Cate said shortly. "Can I take out a restraining order against him?"

Gerald frowned. "He hasn't threatened you in any way?"

"Only to say he wants his son."

Gerald spread his manicured hands. "Fair enough, wouldn't you have said? We have fathers coming in here who've had a very tough time of it. I can't help thinking as a *man* the law as it stands is weighted heavily towards the mother. No wonder these dangerous protests are being staged by fathers. It's a desperate cry for attention."

"I agree." Cate's knees were beginning to shake. "So you're on his side?"

Gerald demurred. "As a lawyer, Cate, I must take a balanced view. Your Julian Carlisle has rights." He paused, the skin of his high forehead wrinkling. "Oddly enough the name rings a bell. Julian Carlisle...Julian Carlisle..." he mused. "I've heard the name, I'm sure, in the past week. No worries, it will come to me."

"I'll make it easy." Cate made the decision. "You'll find out anyway. Julian Carlisle is Lord

Wyndham, the fifth Baron Wyndham. He's in Australia at the moment."

Gerald started to drum his fingernails on the desk top. "This whole business could get into the papers."

"I know that." She wanted to relax, but she couldn't.

"What about your job?" he asked. "Do you want to be in the papers? Hugh Saunders wouldn't like any member of his staff being caught up in legal proceedings, especially custody of a child."

"I'll lose everything before I lose my son." Cate's expression was closed.

"Perhaps you could bring Lord Wyndham here?" Gerald suggested, scrutinising her closely. "The three of us could talk. There has to be an amicable solution to this, Cate. No court will give you sole custody, given the circumstances and the calibre of the man you're up against. You must have cared for him once?"

Cate raised her beautiful light green eyes. "He was the love of my life," she said simply. "They say one person can ruin you for anyone else. They got it right."

"I'm not much of an expert." He gave a faint grimace. Gerald had been divorced ten or more years previously. His wife had remarried soon after the divorce, weirdly enough to a younger clone of Gerald.

"I don't know if I can persuade him to come in here," Cate said. "We parted in anger. Anyway, he does his own thing. I haven't told you the full extent of his mother's interference."

"There's more?" Gerald expelled a breath.

Cate nodded, giving him the full picture.

"When he returned from London, his mother told him I had left a note, basically saying I wanted *out*, it was all too much for me, I was too young. She was a talented artist, very good at sketching. I didn't write any Dear John letter, Gerald. His mother wrote it."

Gerald's brows, black in contrast to his silver hair, lifted. "You're saying she forged it?"

"She made use of her talents," Cate said. "Though I didn't hang around long enough to sight it," she added with bitter regret. "God, I was eighteen. No age at all. I was so naïve I believed her. Ashe had taken himself off to London rather than tell me it was all over."

"And you believed her?" Gerald asked somewhat incredulously. Women in his experience were notorious liars.

Cate nodded. "In a way I was in awe of her. Alicia was a law unto herself."

"You should have stayed." Gerald rolled his Mont Blanc pen in his hands. "Given him a chance to explain."

"I know that *now*, Gerald. I didn't know it then," Cate said with deep regret.

"But surely if he loved you he should have come after you?" Gerald persisted. "Money no object and all that?"

"He believed his mother's version of events. That says it all. The terrible thing is liars regularly get to be believed. Why exactly is that?"

No reply from Gerald.

"They rely on being believed, that's why. The people they talk to *know* they're liars yet they're still believed. It's really weird, like people confessing to crimes they didn't commit. People are seriously flawed. Me included. Alicia backed up her version of events with a forged letter. There are so many versions in life. Different versions. Different viewpoints. A half a dozen people can tell six entirely different stories." She took a deep breath, trying to steady herself. "I'm taking up your time, Gerald. It was very good of you to see me without an appointment. I can't keep your other clients waiting." She gathered up her handbag, then stood up.

"Why don't you put it to him, Cate? Surely Alicia has ceased to matter?"

"Oh, she matters," Cate said.

"She certainly left her mark on you. This is your opportunity to put things straight, Cate."

"Only if he brings in a handwriting expert."

"Okay, let's see what I can do." Gerald pulled out a drawer. "He couldn't do better than Georgie Warbuton. She's the best."

Cate brightened. "I've heard of her. She's a forensic document examiner, isn't she?"

Gerald handed over a business card. "Yes. Legal firms and the police have benefited from her amazing expertise. If there are flaws in the handwriting in your letter, Georgina will find it. Good luck."

"Thanks, Gerald," Cate said with real feeling. "I'll leave a message at his hotel."

"Strike while the iron's hot," Gerald urged. "You could cut out a lot of the angst, if you're prepared to be reasonable, Cate. No need to anger Lord Wyndham further. Give him a chance. At the very least the two of you should talk, with a mediator to hand. We're not just talking about the two of you. There's your boy. You don't want anything ugly around your boy. You said Jules took to him on sight?"

"Of course he did. He must have recognised his father at some subconscious level. I wasn't there."

Armed with Georgina's business card, she made the return journey to the hotel where Ashe was staying. She would leave a message for him at Reception. Outside the luxury hotel she paused a moment to ring Stella on her mobile.

"Hi, I'll be a little late. I've just come from Gerald's office. I need legal advice. Gerald sent you his very kindest regards."

"Dear Gerald," said Stella, very offhand.

"He really cares about you too, Stell," Cate said dryly. "Take my word for it. I'll tell you all about it when I get home."

"Take care, Catrina. Do not endanger yourself or your reputation in any way."

"But I've already done that," Cate said and cut the connection.

Over the years different people, mostly women, had tried their best to sling a little mud in her direction. Murphy Stiller for one. The problem boiled down to one thing. Envy. The belief Catrina Hamilton had unfair advantages over them. Little did they know!

Stepping briskly into the lobby, head down, she almost collided with someone. Surely it was impossible to know who you bumped into with your head down? Only all her senses went into overdrive. Her heart was pounding as hard as the first day she had met him. There had to be some primordial explanation for it. Even when her life was totally different, everything was the same.

"Back to see me?" he said, tempted to bundle her up and carry her off. The urge, however primitive, was irresistible. This was the love of his life. As simple and maybe as destructive as that.

She looked up into his handsome face. "Actually yes. Not to *see* you, but leave you a message."

"How good of you." He took her arm, leading her off to the plush seating area with its glass-topped tables. At this time of the afternoon the area was almost empty. Two smartly dressed matrons were sitting on the central banquet in animated conversation. A glorious arrangement of fig branches, cordyline leaves, lime-green liliums centred with gorgeous ruby-red peonies sat atop the cone-shaped pillar that rose above the banquet.

"Well, what is it?" he asked, courteously pulling out her chair.

Ashe had always had beautiful manners. She had loved him not simply because of his outstanding good looks, his privileged position in life, his confidence. He had other important qualities. He was kind, generous, courteous to everyone, as liberal-minded as his mother had been a class snob.

"Thank you." She sat down, opening up her hand bag to extract the card Gerald had given her. "If you're going to visit a handwriting expert, this woman is the best. She has a doctorate in Psychology but she's a forensic document examiner as well. She's made many appearances in court, big fraud cases, that kind of thing."

His raven head was bent as he stared down at the card.

"Her reputation is impeccable," Cate added for good measure.

"Unlike yours."

"Cheap shot."

Of a sudden his eyes met hers. "Okay, I apologise."

"I never thought I'd hear you say that, Ashe," she said, ultra-controlled, when all she could think was how much she had loved him. Lost him. Yet the magic remained alive. "Have you contacted home?" she asked, aware she was adopting more and more an upper-class English accent. It gave her some sort of bizarre satisfaction.

"I check in every day."

"Good for you. Does your wife know about me?"

He glanced away, then back at her. "That's funny," he said.

"Not too funny, I hope? Let me share the joke. I didn't rate a mention? Didn't some poet say after the great love there were minor ones? Which one was I?"

He didn't answer for a minute. Instead he raised a hand to a circling drinks waiter. "I'm not married, Catrina."

Her voice wouldn't work for her. She had never felt so shocked in her life. She wanted to say something, but couldn't. Her vocal cords weren't working.

"You look like you could use a drink," he said crisply. "Why don't I get us a glass of champagne?"

The suavity of his tone went a way to restoring her. "No—wait."

He ignored her. The waiter promptly arrived. He ordered. "I think you can have *one* glass without going over the limit."

"When were you going to tell me?"

"I *have* told you," he said, pretending to be taken aback. "Sometimes it's better not to do everything at once."

Her heart in her chest felt cramped. "I don't understand this. I'm twenty-six, that makes you—"

"Thirty-one," he supplied with a downward drag on his handsome mouth.

"You've never *thought* of getting married? I mean, you have to produce an heir, don't you? It's mandatory."

His eyes flashed. "I could tell you to go to hell, but since you ask, Catrina, I did *once* think of marriage. I already have an heir. Our son, Julian, is my heir."

Something in his tone turned her blood ice-cold. "I'll never deliver him up to you."

"Never say never," he warned.

The most shocking aspect was, some part of her was *rejoicing*. Ashe wasn't married. What did that make her? *Human, perhaps?* Ashe hadn't married

Marina or what was her name—Talia, Tallis? She ought to say something.

He was the one to speak. "All these years wasted," he said. "But I guess it's a part of life."

"I'm not the only one to blame, Ashe." She put up a hand as though to tidy her already immaculately arranged blonde hair.

"That's just it," he said, like a stab. "You carry your own share of blame."

"Maybe, but I was too inexperienced and you weren't there. I believed your mother, Ashe. Just as you did. Your mother destroyed our relationship. Go see the handwriting expert. I can provide you with samples for comparison."

His hand suddenly shot out to grasp her narrow wrist. How warm her skin was. How satiny smooth. How sizzling the contact. He would never get over the craving to touch her. "You could doctor them."

Anger swept through her. Anger and a never-ending hunger. It was like living with a powerful addiction. "Careful, our drinks are coming," he warned.

The waiter duly arrived, delivering two glasses of champagne with a smile.

"Drink up, Catrina," Wyndham said, after the waiter had gone. "I can't stay long."

"Neither can I," she returned sharply. "I have to get home."

"To our boy? Tell me, what was really behind Stella's decision to emigrate to Australia? People have been talking about it for years. She could easily have adopted a child in England. Instead she left her home, her family, everyone she knew. It doesn't make sense. Not then. Not now."

"It doesn't have to, does it? They made their decision. Their lives. Let it lie."

The flame in his blue eyes flared up. "Only I'm not prepared to let anything lie."

"In that case you'll have the note examined by an expert who could study recent and old examples of my writing. I have journals I kept from years ago." Only she wouldn't want anyone sighting them. They were far too personal, too private. "Cheers," she said ironically, picking up her glass and taking a long drink, her mouth filling with bubbles.

"I ought to tell you I kept some old examples of your handwriting myself," he admitted.

She gave a sceptical laugh. "You're not going to tell me on your person?"

"I have copies," he replied, unperturbed by the taunt. "Olivia will send the originals."

"So you mean to have the letter tested?" She was lured into hope.

"I will if you come with me." The hardness was still in his voice. "If you allow me to see my son."

Cate experienced another moment of panic.

"Invite me for lunch at the weekend," he suggested.

"You don't belong in our world."

"I think otherwise. I'm sure our son will be happy to see me. My regards to Stella. I must tell the family I'm delighted to have found her after all these years."

It would all come out now. She was sure of it. But Annabel was dead. "Did any of them actually come to Australia to look her up?" she challenged.

"Well, of course her sister did, the notorious Annabel."

Cate bridled. "Notorious?"

"Keep calm. Annabel was somewhat on the wild side, I believe. At least that was the word. Her marriage to Warren was a farce. It suited him to have a beautiful young wife. Annabel apparently got in with a fast lot. Drink, drugs, the usual thing. I wouldn't really know. Before my time. I do know she came out to Australia, didn't she, that final time?"

"I don't want to talk about Annabel," Cate said, shaking her head. "The woman is dead."

"So is my mother. Actually no one wants to talk about Annabel," he said. "A distant cousin of mine was madly in love with her at some phase of his young life."

The question flew out of her mouth. "And who

was that?" This was her best chance of finding something out.

"Why do you want to know?" His glance sharpened.

"Excuse me for asking."

"It was a Ralph Stewart. Everyone called him Rafe. He was a friend of my father's."

"Was?" Cate noted the past tense. She had never heard of the man until very recently yet the news came as a heart-stopper.

"Why the interest?" he asked, leaning forward a little.

She had made a mistake with the intensity of tone. "I'm making conversation."

"Fine, except you sound like you really want to know." He sat back. "Rafe is very much alive. He's a prominent political figure. It's my father who is no longer with us."

"I regret I didn't know him," Cate offered quietly. Geoffrey Carlisle's tragic end was a subject never broached.

"Had he lived he would have inherited the title and all that went with it," he said.

"*Stella* should have," Cate, the feminist, shot back.

"I agree, but all the large estates were entailed. It was a protective measure. Only males could inherit, the original idea being to keep the land in the family. You do see the sense of it? Sisters marry into other families. Stella and her sister, Annabel, were handsomely provided for. The title and land passed to me."

"Are you sure Jules could be your heir?" she asked with some sarcasm. "He's that quaint term—illegitimate. That could disrupt your plans."

"Nothing will disrupt my plans," he said and meant it. "Julian will not lose out."

"And I'll never let him go, Ashe," she responded fiercely. "I'll fight tooth and claw for him. You'll never take him off to England. He won't want to go. You'd better take that into account. Jules is an Australian, Ashe. He loves his own country. As do I. This issue will go to litigation. I've already consulted a solicitor."

She spoke with the inner toughness of a woman who had pride and confidence in herself. He couldn't help but admire her effrontery. "Won't do you a bit of good," he said. "You're heavily in my debt, Catrina. You knowingly and willingly deprived me of all knowledge of my son. Now you've come up with a last-ditch attempt at mitigation."

"If I give you my promise you can see my son you will see Georgina Warbuton?"

"*Our* son," he corrected. "He has your blond hair but as he gets older the Carlisle physical characteristics will emerge. He's tall for his age, well built. That cute nose will form into my *beak*, as you used to call it. He already has the Carlisle eyes. Stella would confirm that." He tapped the glass-topped table hard. "There's something all wrong here," he declared.

"Like what?" What she was feeling was alarm. Even her breathing was audible.

"My mother used to say you reminded her of someone." He stared across at her.

"Now that's just not believable. I was born here."

"You have your adoption papers?"

He held her eyes so she couldn't look down. "Of course I have," she scoffed. "They're nothing to do with you."

"You are the mother of my child." He was gravely intent on her.

"Well I wasn't good enough for you then—why go into my ancestry? There could well be a convict lurking in *my* biological family's tree."

He was still watching her. "Your biological mother could well be alive."

"She isn't." She'd had enough of this questioning.

"How do you know?" he shot back very fast.

"I checked. Don't know who my biological father was. Sorry. Can't help you there."

"And Stella applied for adoption here in Australia?"

She forced herself to stay calm. "Do I have to

spell it out? Stella couldn't have children of her own. What else could she do? She wanted a new life. She wanted a child. That child was me. She's been a wonderful mother to me and grandmother to Jules."

His expression softened slightly. "I could see how devoted they are to each other." There was a deep tender sadness in his tone. "But there's a story here, Catrina." He looked directly at her. "And I'm going to find it out."

"Fine!" She threw up her head. "Pity you weren't like that years ago." Her voice bit so deep he almost flinched.

"One thing I am is *responsible*, Catrina," he replied. "I would have thought you knew that. I would have taken full responsibility for you and our child. I would have married you just as we planned. Correction—as *I* planned."

Catrina stood up, leaving the rest of the champagne in her glass untouched. "Well, it took your mother to sabotage your plans. I'll make the appointment to see Georgina Warbuton. I'll let you know when."

He too rose to his feet. "It had better be soon. I want to see Julian at the weekend." He glanced at his watch. "I have an appointment to keep."

"Don't let me hold you up."

"I'll walk you to your car."

"Don't bother." Strain was in her voice. "It's parked nearly a block away."

"No problem. I have time."

Out on the busy street he took her arm as they threaded their way through the crowd. She could feel the energy coming off his body. His subtle masculine cologne was in her nostrils. Ashe had some power, no other man in her life, and she had known quite a few very attractive men, had made her feel so female. So much the *Woman*. A woman to be greatly desired. He was Jules' father. The last thing she wanted was a viciously fought child-custody battle. It could destroy her and his well-ordered world. But the most important person in all this was Jules.

Their son.

CHAPTER EIGHT

WITH GERALD'S RECOMMENDATION Cate was able to make an after-hours appointment with Georgina Warbuton, who was on call as an expert witness in a current hot case involving massive fraud.

She picked up Ashe outside his hotel. He was waiting on the pavement, looking out for her car. He got in quickly, shut the door, effectively locking them in together. He looked very handsome in a mustard-coloured jacket, blue jeans, with a midnight-blue cotton shirt open at the throat. She felt her body go into insubordinate surges of desire. If this were a romance novel she'd be flinging herself at him with primitive abandon. Only this was real life.

"Seat belt," she prompted, not looking at him. Wiser to keep her eye on the traffic. Mother Nature had given Ashe far too many advantages.

"I do know how to do this," he pointed out. He slung the belt across him and locked it in. "Nice car."

"Thank you." He had made no comment the last time he was in it. "I have an excellent high-paying job."

"I know exactly how much you get," he said very dryly.

Cate was angered. "I beg your pardon." She flashed him an irate glance.

"It would be a good idea to watch the road," he said as a white Porsche pulled out right in front of them.

"I can't believe Hugh gave that away." Hugh was exceedingly discreet.

"It wasn't Hugh."

"Tell me. I want to know."

He glanced at her. She had a beautiful profile. He hadn't been celibate all these years, but just looking at Catrina was a bigger turn-on than full-blown sex with any other woman in all that time. Catrina was the real thing. A *femme fatale.* "You understand envy," he said. "I understand envy. People become envious. It's the way of the world."

"It was Murphy Stiller?"

He gave an exaggerated sigh. "I don't want to go into it. Settlement date for Isla Bella is ninety days hence. Thank you for your part in it."

"Lady McCready liked you. She's no snob, but Lord Wyndham did the trick. And then of course she knows about the trainloads of money. But surely you won't have the time for frequent visits?"

"I'll find time," he said. "Trustworthy caretakers are in place. They'll look after it for me. I'll allow my family and friends to use the island. You may even rate an invite. Julian certainly will."

"Jules won't go anywhere without me," she said sharply.

"Then you can come too."

All her resources, mind and body, were being put to work. "Oh, God, Ashe," she breathed. "Isn't ours a star-crossed story?"

He considered that for a long moment. "There's been far too much anguish, Catrina. I don't believe in love stories any more."

She felt tears come into her eyes. She blinked them away. "Do you have my notes with you?" she asked.

"Two samples. The ones we can actually use. The others were a bit too personal. One would have thought you were desperately in love with me."

"I was. For a time." Occasionally one had to tell lies.

"It must have been difficult forgetting you ever cared?" he asked with a terrible calm.

"How was it for you?" She shot him a sparkling glance.

"I saw it as horrible treachery."

"On the basis of what your mother told you, then showed you. That's why we're going to consult Georgina Warbuton. I should warn you, you won't be able to go on exonerating your mother. I know how painful that will be. You can't claim total ignorance either. You knew your mother was dead set on Marina."

Knowledge of that was hitting him increasingly hard. He remained silent.

"Sorry, Ashe," said Cate. "Your mother had no conscience when it came to you and what she thought you should have. A different value system came into play."

Georgina Warbuton couldn't have been kinder, or nicer. A handsome woman in her late fifties, she welcomed them into her elegant terraced home. A tall, distinguished-looking man she introduced as her husband. After a few pleasantries, her husband left them.

They were offered tea, coffee, politely refused. Both of them were intent on getting answers. Georgina Warbuton shepherded them into her book-lined study, more like a library with floor-to-ceiling built-in bookcases on either side of a marble fireplace. A lovely flower painting of the Dutch school—it appeared to have been done with a palette knife—hung over it. The polished floor was covered with a beautiful vibrant Persian rug in deep reds and blues. There was room for a comfortable sofa and two matching armchairs covered

in a beautiful blue silk-velvet picking up the colour
in the rug and the blue of Ashe's shirt.

Dr Warbuton waited until they were seated before she took the sensitive documents into her
long, expressive hands. Her keen gaze was very
serious now. She was fully occupied with what
was before her. "This shouldn't take long," she announced after a few moments, retreating behind
her antique desk. There she switched on a table
light with a strong beam, angling it towards her.
Next she began to delve in a desk drawer.

To Cate, desperately hopeful, that sounded as
though Dr Warbuton thought the outcome was a
foregone conclusion.

Vindication.

For a moment her spirits soared, then crashed
back to earth again.

Too late.

Cate looked over at the man she still loved. His
hands were locked. He was looking down, his
lean, athletic body perfectly still. For a split second she wanted to move across to him on the sofa,
hold his hand. He had viewed Alicia with the eyes
of a loving son. Blood was thicker than water.

Georgina Warbuton was examining the documents very closely now. Whatever she thought
she was keeping quiet about it until she was absolutely sure.

There *couldn't* be a problem. There couldn't,

Cate thought with a sinking feeling of dismay. Even the greatest art experts in the world had been tricked. Had Alicia been so clever she had even fooled an expert?

Finally Dr Warbuton looked up, her gaze intense. "It is my professional opinion, this letter—" she held up the contentious note "—is not the handwriting of Catrina here. It is in fact a clever forgery." Her voice was dispassionate, but her eyes were kind.

"You're absolutely sure?" Ashe asked gravely.

"I am." Dr Warbuton's answer was quiet. "If the matter is so very important to you, you could consult another handwriting expert, but they will tell you the same thing. If you care to come here I can show you various markers."

Cate shook her head. She didn't want to see them. She didn't want to augment Ashe's pain. She looked to him as he sat mute.

Georgina Warbuton gave them both a moment. She could see how tremendously important verification of the document was. She had no doubt at all it had been carefully written by a hand other than the beautiful young woman in front of her. A clever hand. An artist's hand? The purpose? It was none of her business. She had to be entirely objective in her judgments.

Finally Ashe rose to his feet, his striking features taut. It was obvious he was feeling deep emotion. "That won't be necessary, Dr Warbuton," he said, respect in his voice. "You're a recognised expert in these matters. We won't proceed further."

Out in the street again she had to near run to keep pace with him, her face thrown up against the breeze, a strand of her hair coming loose, whipping across her cheek. Her body was humming with high-pitched nervous energy. Ashe's broad back, the set of his square shoulders, indicated he was battling a heavy load of tension.

He reached the car before she did.

"Are you getting in?" she asked, staring up into his taut face.

He touched an elegant hand to his temple. "I don't think so. I feel like walking."

"You don't know this part of the city," she said. "You could get lost. It's a long haul back to your hotel."

"I can always catch a cab," he said curtly.

"Please, Ashe." She tried to force balance, reason, into her voice. "I know you're upset."

He suddenly reached for her bare slender arms, clutching them hard. *"Upset?"* The expression on his handsome face was ravaged. "You were right!"

"Let me go, Ashe," she said quietly.

He released her with a sharp jerk. "God," he groaned. "Not one of us doubted her. Olivia, Leonie, me. We accepted her word, totally."

Cate, a mother herself, was now closer to understanding. "She was your mother, the strongest force in your life. The woman who had taken care of you from your very first breath. Your father wasn't there to make a judgment. I'm sure he would have handled things better."

"I can't answer that," he said, when he knew that would definitely have been the case. His father had been a highly intelligent man with wide-ranging briefs in very important work.

"You told me once your mother and father didn't agree on lots of things?" she suggested.

"My father saw things a whole lot clearer than my mother." His answer was brusque. "She tended to get very emotional."

"Not the best state to be in when you're trying to make an objective judgment. We all know that. Why don't you get in the car?" she urged. "I'll drive you back to the hotel."

They were well under way. But she hadn't composed herself sufficiently to take the next obstacle on board.

"Okay, my mother did a very wrong thing," he acknowledged tersely. "She had allowed herself to believe *my* life was hers. But *you*! I told you over and over I loved you deeply, Catrina. You were precious to me. You were part of my life; the whole twin souls bit. I told you I wanted to *share* my life with you. Yet you forgot all that the moment I turned my back."

"I was *young*, Ashe. Too young. Just a kid. You were five years older. Had I been five years older I may have handled it better. But your mother tied me up in knots. We both did the wrong thing. If your mother convinced *you*, think what an effect she had on me."

He shoved a hand through his wind-tousled hair. "You could have given yourself time to think it all through. I was home two days later. You could have stayed."

The sharp edges in his voice cut into her. "Ashe, I was told to back off in no uncertain terms. I really don't want this conversation. It's all too late."

"No, it isn't. I'm right *here*, Catrina, physically beside you. How many times did we make love?" he asked, in what seemed to her a totally disillusioned voice.

"One time too many," she said, then immediately shook her head. "I can't say that. I have my Jules."

"*Our* Jules," he said right on cue. "I just wish you'd told me. God knows you've had years."

The extraordinary thing was, in retrospect she had to ask herself why hadn't she? "The reason— or one of the reasons—was I believed you were married; probably had a couple of kids. I only had Jules. Please, Ashe. Just let it lie."

"I know my obligations," he said firmly.

They were nearing the hotel, one of the finest five-star hotels in the city. It was stunningly situated, overlooking the Harbour and the Opera House. "There's a parking spot. Grab it."

"I'm not coming in," she said briefly. Even with the air conditioning on, the interior of the car was steaming up.

"Grab it," he repeated in a crisp, authoritative tone. Ashe had come a long way over the past years. He was no longer the young man she had known.

She felt far too agitated to argue. She had caught the flash in his eyes.

Inside the hotel he steered her seemingly solicitously towards the bank of lifts. "We have a custody agreement to work out."

"We have *no* custody agreement," she muttered, playing her part. "I want my son full time. I won't share him."

He only gave one of his elegant shrugs. "Neither of us wants to cause him grief. He's my son, too, Catrina. I would think your solicitor pointed this out to you. You've had Julian for the past seven years. It's your turn to make it up to me."

"So what do you want?" She was aware her

emotions were getting out of hand. Always the see-saw. Up and down.

"Maybe we should talk about this in my suite," he said, lowering his voice as several hotel guests approached the lifts.

They were inside his spacious suite on the thirty-fourth floor. It was decorated in a sophisticated style with rich silks and exotic Honduran mahogany, but the emphasis was on comfort. There was a splendid view of the city's icons all aglitter through the series of triple-glazed soundproofed plate-glass windows.

"Sit down," he said, extending a hand towards one of the three-seater sofas, luxuriously upholstered.

"All I can give you is a half hour," she said, smoothing the skirt of her sleeveless silk cotton dress, printed in a medley of green and gold.

A black eyebrow shot up. "A half hour? That's it?"

"I have a lot of work lined up for tomorrow, Ashe. A good thing Hugh is handling your affairs himself."

"I suppose he would as he's the boss," he said dryly. "Want a drink?" He walked to the mini-bar.

"No," she answered. "Maybe a Perrier water."

He gave her a taut half smile. "Coming up. I'm

not going to waive my right to see Julian at the weekend."

Cate felt herself stiffen. "You're not going to say anything to him?"

"As a matter of fact—" He made her wait until he had poured her a mineral water.

"As a matter of fact, *what*?" She was on tenterhooks.

"Of course I'm not going to say anything," he said, coming back towards her. "We both know the time isn't right."

"Is it *ever* going to be right, Ashe? I doubt it." She looked and felt unspeakably sad. Most of the previous night she had lain awake wondering what his plans would be. At such times her mind inevitably going back over the halcyon days they had spent together. The long walks, the conversations they'd had. They had talked about their hopes and their dreams, about art, literature, movies, religion, philosophy, politics, floated theories. They could talk about anything and find it immensely enjoyable. Both of them were born scholars always out to learn. Ashe had read Law and Economics at Oxford, graduating with a double first. If he had been thinking of following his father into British Intelligence, his father's death had made him rethink his plans.

He bent to put his glass down on the coffee table between the two sofas, then he shouldered out of his jacket, placing it over one of six chairs set around a glass-topped table in the dining area. Another lovely arrangement of flowers sat on the coffee table; a low celadon-coloured bowl of perfect velvety white gardenias that spread their ravishing perfume. No doubt they would be replaced the following day as they wilted but for now the blooms were astonishingly beautiful. Cate resisted the impulse to stroke a velvety petal. She didn't want to discolour it, though her own luminous skin looked just as stroke-able.

"You always did like white flowers," he said, taking a seat opposite her. "The rose gardens at the hall are quite famous now. People come from all over to view them on open days. I seem to remember your favourites. Snow Queen was one. It's one of the great roses, then there was the profusely flowering Iceberg—"

"And that wonderfully fragrant Bride," she broke in, fancying she could almost smell the perfume of the beautiful large, pure white rose with its exquisite form.

"There's a walled garden devoted entirely to white roses," he told her. "My idea. No need to ask what had prompted it," he said with some irony.

She looked up and their eyes locked. Always the quickening sensations in her body, the thrum of electricity. She *knew* the same electrical current was switched on in him. It was something neither of them seemed able to control. The very air was sexualised, exciting. "Cate," he murmured, "tell me this didn't happen. None of it happened."

The regret in his voice was echoed in her own. "I wish I could. I told you, we're star-crossed lovers."

"No one could take your place."

That cut to her heart, yet she said crisply, "And I bet there was no shortage of candidates. You'll find an eligible woman, Ashe, close to your rank."

His blue eyes burned. "Do stop talking rubbish. Prince William married his Kate. Prince Frederik married his Mary. Two great romances. My mother's mindset was from another time."

"God, Ashe, she was only in her mid-fifties then. Maybe she was channelling Queen Victoria?"

"Our present Queen had to marry a prince, or at the very least an earl. Ironic, isn't it? How times change. Princess Margaret couldn't marry her divorced airman. Hard to believe now but it happened and she suffered."

"Your lot are still as stuffy," she said.

He frowned, although he knew in many cases it was true. "There's got to be a plausible explanation for Stella Radclyffe—your adopted mother, so you say—taking off for the other side of the world. She didn't attend her own father's funeral. Needless to say that was seized upon. Whereas Annabel, the supposed flighty one, was there. Decidedly odd. It wouldn't come as much of a surprise to me to find out *Annabel* was your biological mother." He looked surprised by his own observation.

Cate sprang to her feet. "That is so...so..."

"*Possible*. Sit down, Cate," he said with crisp authority. "I will get the answers, although I believe I've got one now. How's this for a hypothesis? Annabel fell pregnant. It would have created a great scandal at the time. She was unmarried, very young, pampered and adored. So what scheme did the sisters hatch?"

"I'm not following you at all." Of course she was. She resumed her seat, but pointedly glanced at her watch. Her heart was racing.

"No, you're not following me, you're way ahead. Always something to hide. That's you, isn't it, Catrina? When did you find out?" The blunt question was like a lash.

Of a sudden Cate gave up the deceit, torn by rage and shame. She was sick of it all, half frightened too. "Annabel came to visit Stella to be with someone who loved her and there to die. She had burned herself out."

"Sadly she did," he agreed in a sympathetic tone.

"But before she died she made a deathbed confession. She needed to get on the right side of the Big Guy up there. *She* was my biological mother.

She had begged Stella to save her and her reputation. Big sister Stella came to the rescue, sacrificing herself. My mother didn't want me, you know," she said and tried to smile. "A baby would have sabotaged her plans."

Of course. That was it.

Ashe looked into her face, seeing a lifetime of tremendous hurt and pain of rejection. Pain of rejection gave credence to her story. Here was the mother of his child, living a large part of her life thinking herself an adopted child only to discover as a woman she had been deceived by someone who loved her, her own aunt, Stella. There would be long-reaching consequences of this.

"You must have been shocked, more at Stella than Annabel. Why didn't Stella tell you at some point much earlier?"

Cate rested her blonde head back on the sofa. "To be honest, I don't think she could get it out. I used to think I would never forgive her for not telling me."

"And have you? I'd say you still haven't forgiven her. Maybe you never will."

A sad smile was etched on Cate's face. "Bitterness taints, Ashe. I love Stella. She's my aunt, and Jules' great-aunt. She spent a lifetime looking out for her little sister and then looking after me."

"Did Annabel never reveal who your father is?"

He could see tears behind the sparkle in her eyes, veiled by her long lashes.

"Maybe she didn't *know*." Her lovely mouth firmed into a disillusioned smile.

"Oh, she *knew*," Ashe retorted. "It's up to you now to find out."

It was such an effort to keep her voice steady. "I don't want to know either."

"I don't accept that. Your biological father may well have been in the same position as me." Ashe's tone hardened. "Have you ever considered Annabel mightn't have told him?"

She felt a sudden chill as though Annabel's shade were right behind her. "I have no idea. Both you and Stella have made the comment Rafe Stewart was madly in love with Annabel at the time. Do you recall anything your mother or father might have said?"

"Not in front of me or my sisters," he said. "We were kids. Rafe is, as I said, a prominent politician."

She stared at the area rug. "Is he married? I'm not saying there could be any connection, just asking the question."

"He's married, yes. To Helena Stewart, a lovely woman. She runs a very successful interior-decorating business."

"Children?"

He didn't answer. He appeared to be battling feelings of his own.

"Is that a no, then?" The room seemed very quiet now, as though the walls were listening.

"They had an only child, a son, Martin," he said finally. "Martin was a bit of a playboy. He was very handsome, very charming, very droll. But he was always in some kind of trouble with Rafe having to bail him out. He went into rehabilitation a number of times. Everyone hoped he'd beat his addiction, but in the end he died of an overdose. It took both Rafe and Helena years to pull out of it. Somehow they did."

Cate felt utter dismay. "How very, very tragic. What would have made a young man with everything in life become dependent on drugs?"

Ashe shrugged. "Once they start they can't stop. It's a tough world out there for young people these days. The availability, the peer pressure. Sometimes it must get so oppressive they feel driven to conform. Martin felt he lived very much in his father's shadow. He had the morbid fear he could never measure up, never meet the high expectations he thought were expected of him. His own harsh judgment, I have to tell you. His parents loved him. He was sent down from Oxford. He and another one of his druggie pals. Rich kids. It was all downhill from there. His sense of self-esteem gave out."

"It upset you, didn't it?"

"It greatly upset everyone who knew him. Death is no victory, no way out. What it was, was a tragic waste of a young life."

She could see he was still trying to grapple with Martin Stewart's death. "What did he look like?" she asked after a long moment, because somehow it seemed right.

Ashe exhaled heavily. "The girls used to call him Adonis. He was very handsome, as I said, but he settled for looking *louche*. That was the image he wanted to project." He was speaking now as though under a spell. "Martin had thick blond hair that he wore quite long." He touched his shoulders as an indicator. "He had lots of 'friends' but no close friends. The real friends were very worried about him. They tried to help him so he cut them out of his life. His so called 'friends' brought out the worst in him. But that was where he wanted to stay although it was a life sentence."

"I'm so sorry," Cate said. "I can only guess at the agony of his parents and his friends. Wasn't it Aristotle who said: The gods had no greater torment than for a mother to lose her child?"

"He might have said *father* too," Ashe answered for the fathers of the world.

"Maybe mothers have the edge in suffering? Not everyone has the strength to fight for life. To some, it must seem easier to throw it away."

He nodded grimly, looked away.

"Tell me something, Ashe." She felt compelled to forge ahead. "Do *I* resemble him at all?" Her question was calm enough but her heart was beating too fast for comfort.

"Sorry?" The sound of her voice brought him out of his reverie.

"Do *I* look like Martin? Straightforward question."

"God, Catrina!" He found himself staring back at her as though looking for enlightenment from above. Realisation began to press in on him. He had thought he was beyond surprise. Hadn't her colouring always struck him as familiar? She wasn't a copy of Martin, but she certainly could have been his sister!

"Hello, Ashe!" She wanted to jolt him into speech. "At least it's not a *hell no*!"

"Catrina, this is all too strange." The expression on his handsome face was both proud and moody. "If I said yes, I could be putting you on the wrong track entirely. Why don't you discuss it with Stella? That woman knows the story. Maybe the *whole* story. She would never have laid eyes on Martin, but she did know Rafe and as far as I recall she went to school with Rafe's sister, Penelope."

The veiled attack on Stella wasn't lost on her.

"Stella has hardly said a blessed thing about either of them."

"She is without doubt a very secretive woman." Even a ruthless woman. Ashe's gaze was intense and highly speculative.

"This is an odd conversation we're having." Cate too was feeling decidedly uneasy.

"Well, it is *odd*, isn't it? Stella migrating to Australia to save her younger sister's reputation; refusing to acknowledge your true relationship, claiming she adopted you, presumably from an agency. Pretty hard to plead that down to a misdemeanour."

The misdemeanours were beginning to pile up. "She's very sorry for it now," Cate said.

"Maybe she could purge her sorrow telling you the truth?" he suggested crisply.

"Maybe it's too bad to tell—ever thought of that? I never questioned Stella, you know. I was always aware I looked *different*. Both Stella and Annabel had dark hair and dark eyes. Things might have been different had I been a carbon copy of my biological mother. As I'm not, I must take after my father. Whoever he may be," she said gravely. "You've experienced firsthand what deception can do, Ashe, your own mother forging a letter. People do it all the time. Letters, documents, anything where they have something to gain. Anyway—"

she rose with determination to her feet "—I didn't come here to rehash the past."

"Then why *did* you come?" His blue eyes burned over her.

"You already know. *One*, you more or less compelled me. *Two*, so I could fix a time for you to see Jules. In my company, of course."

"Do you really think I'm going to jump on a plane with him?" he returned very dryly.

She made a mock face of apology.

"Actually I'd like to spend the whole day with him. Maybe this coming Sunday? We could go for a drive, have lunch somewhere. The Hunter Valley isn't all that far away, is it? The Blue Mountains boat trip on the Harbour? One could never tire of seeing it from the water. Or as a seven-year-old Julian might like a trip to Taronga Park Zoo. I understand the location is fantastic with the best vantage points on Sydney Harbour. Maybe we can leave it to Julian to choose."

"We call him *Jules*," she said. Julian seemed to mark him as Ashe's son.

Ashe too was on his feet. He had moved too close to her, causing a swift reaction. Her heart was beating like a bird imprisoned in her chest.

"His *father* calls him Julian," he said in a voice that would have crushed another woman. But not Cate. "We can introduce the Jules later as we get to know each other." He had moved even nearer

The space between them was thrumming with heat. "So what time Sunday?"

"Ooh…" Something further was coming. "Nine suit you? I think Jules would like the zoo."

"Then the zoo it is," he said with just a touch of mockery.

She knew she mustn't touch him. Or he touch her. She knew she was only kidding herself. "Goodnight, Ashe."

"Goodnight, Catrina." He caught her wrist, twisted his fingers around it. "I'll come with you to your car." His eyes were full of strange lights.

"No need." Holding her hand, he had to register her whole body as drawn as taut as a wire. She felt as hot as if she were coming down with a fever.

"I've no intention of letting you go alone. A beautiful woman on her own is a target for unwanted attention."

"I've never had any trouble. *Really*, Ashe." She was in far more trouble where she was.

"Why sound so edgy? As much as part of me hates to admit it, I want to keep you beside me for ever."

"You sound like you're in crisis," she taunted. "You despise your own weakness."

"Don't you have the same problem?" he challenged, a note of cynicism creeping in.

"I've learned my lesson, Ashe. It wouldn't work. Then or now." She shifted away a fraction.

"Sure you didn't write that note?" He lifted an indolent hand to remove the pretty art-nouveau clasp that held back her hair. "There, doesn't that feel better?" he asked, unrepentant, as her beautiful hair, set free, slid forward in a smooth motion.

"You can't take that clip," she protested. "It's an antique piece." He had put it in his pocket.

"I'll give it back," he said. "Promise."

There was such an extraordinary aura about him, a whole catalogue of advantages, the natural authority, the seeming calm and underneath a huge reserve of passion. It was shattering to know even if she wanted to, she couldn't break her bond with him.

"I don't know what we're doing here, Ashe, but if it's a ploy to soften me up, it won't work. You can't take Jules. My son is my life." The tremulous note in her voice gave her away.

"What if I take you as well?" he suggested, staring down at her in such a way it fired her blood. "Like it or not Julian is part of us both. What do you think he would say if you told him I was his father? Told him how circumstance ripped us apart. Told him how I lived to marry you, to make you my wife? What would he say if I told him when my back was turned, you vanished out of my life never to tell me *or* him we are father and son."

Of a sudden her nerve failed, ebbed away. "This is emotional blackmail, Ashe."

"I don't care what it is," he returned bluntly. "It's the *truth*."

"Jules is not ready for the truth, Ashe," she cried, knowing she was becoming overexcited. "I was wrong to come here."

A shadow crossed his handsome face. "But you've been wrong all along. I'm not going to give up my son, Catrina." There was a quiet but deadly firmness in his voice.

Colour rose beneath her skin as he confirmed her own thought. She turned on him, racked by conflicting emotions. "So where is it all going to end?"

He looked at her sharply weighing that up. "Don't you feel *some* guilt?" Anger spilled from eyes that were bluer than any Burmese sapphire.

"If we're going to make denunciations, what about *you*?" she hit back incautiously. "I'd say we're about even when it comes to making mistakes."

"Okay, okay." He partly agreed. "Only my plan is to put it right. You're not married. Neither am I. In a sense our lives were blown apart. Now I want you back in my life again. You're the mother of my son. I remind you that you were born of an English mother and almost certainly an English father. Don't you remember how you fitted in? You didn't think you would, but you did. The English side of you came to the fore. Julian's long vacation is coming up. May I make a suggestion? You could think about spending Christmas in England with me. You and Julian, Stella too if she wants to come. I would think she would like to return to her birthplace."

"What, as a visitor?" she retorted hotly when she felt a wave of near-happy anticipation. "Stella and my mother were born at Radclyffe Hall, Ashe. But *you* got it all. So does that mean you get to make all the decisions too?"

"Go file a complaint," he said caustically. "It was all legal, Catrina. *Your* grandfather, might I point out, made me his heir. Of course it would have been my father, but I was next in line. Julian one day may very well be the sixth Baron Wyndham. You can't change that."

"Try me!" She threw up her head. "Jules has already confided his ambition to anyone who will listen. He's aiming to become Prime Minister of Australia. He wants to put things right. He wants to be in a position to make life better for everyone. He won't change. He won't turn into an upper-class English boy packed off to boarding school as soon as he can toddle."

Ashe heard the conviction in her voice. He had to face the fact she could be right about their son and his long-term aims. He had fallen in love with Cate, reared in Australia where life was very open, confident and remarkably frank. Hadn't she been different from all the other girls in his circle?

"Understand me clearly," he said. "What Julian wants is important to me as well. I would never force a decision on him. But you've had our son for the past seven years. I am going to redress that. You can make it easy, or you can make it hard. It's up to you."

"So what roles do we play?" She swallowed with difficulty.

"I'll tell my sisters quietly all they need to know."

"I doubt they can keep it to themselves." She managed a derisory laugh.

"We *all* have experience of keeping things to ourselves, Catrina. You would know that better than most. Julian is their nephew, therefore they will do everything to protect him."

"In effect what I'm seeing is a Carlisle take-over."

His eyes flashed. "I'm not saying that at all, Catrina. I'm saying nothing concrete at the moment."

It was crisis point. The breath shook in her throat as she said, "But you will. When and if you do get to know more about Jules you might have to forfeit at least some of your plans. Since Jules was born I have been solely responsible for him."

"Because you omitted to inform me, his father," he shot back, rather bleakly.

That omission now hurt her. She strained away from him, but he held her fast.

"Cate!" he groaned.

She felt her heart constrict. "What happens if he doesn't like you and your family?"

"That's the worst possible scenario. Have you enough grace to accord me some understanding on this?"

"Not yet." He was moving much too fast. "Don't make me hate you, Ashe."

"I think I can handle it." His smile held a degree of self-mockery. "Besides you don't hate me at all. Life has caught up with us, Cate."

"But I'm not the Cate I used to be. Poor vulnerable little Cate. I'm *another* me. I have *another* life."

He had the sense he had a tigress by the tail. "Your *life* was supposed to be with me. Remember what you called it—*destiny.*"

He had touched a psychic nerve. "Destiny did a darn good job of mucking us up."

Within seconds their confrontation had moved from a kind of maddened frustration to a violent need to come together. To physically connect. There were layers upon layers of yearning beneath the conflict that was at best only skin deep.

"What I want to do now—what I *need* to do now is kiss you," he said in a voice seductive with want. His eyes devoured her face, came to rest on her mouth. "Your mouth is no different from what it used to be, do you know that? It's perfect. Perfect for me. Perfect for kissing. God, I couldn't count the kisses." His arms enfolded her, one hand very firm at her back.

Her whole body was pierced with awareness. "What is *this* going to solve, Ashe?" She knew where they were inexorably heading.

"That neither of us are going to fall in love with anyone else?"

"We've still got time." Only residual pride allowed her to say that.

"A lifetime won't be long enough for either of us to forget. I finally have you, Cate."

He looked down at her with intensity. He was mesmerising her and she was letting him. The effect was spine-tingling. "You think you do."

"I *know* I do," he said in his resonant voice. "The image of you has stayed with me. Cate, the eighteen-year-old girl, ravishingly pretty, now a true beauty. The fine bone structure of your face is more apparent. Your skin is as translucent as porcelain."

She knew she could have pulled away. Ashe would never handle her roughly. Only she stood there, held by his hypnotic gaze.

"Did you ever just once *mean* you loved me?" he asked as though he was trying to make sense of it all.

"I don't want to go back that far," she pleaded. Everything was totally different. Everything was the same.

"Let me remind you." He tipped up her chin, only to trail a line of kisses over her cheek to behind her ear. His mouth moved lower to nuzzle her neck, sending thrill after thrill shooting through her. How had she ever thought she could stop caring? His roving mouth came to rest in the warm hollow above her collarbone. "Remember this?" he asked dreamily.

She felt the coaxing caress of his hand. "Maybe…" Her voice shook. There was more to come. Nothing she could or would do to stop it. She was locked into a spell. She never had been able to withstand the spells Ashe wove. She was programmed to respond.

His mouth came down over hers, almost but not quite kissing her. "Seven long years," he muttered. "Misery for me. But a great thing happened to you, didn't it, Cate? You had our son." He pulled her in very tightly as though she would never be free to go.

A warm languor was sweeping through her, robbing her legs of strength. She had an idea she was leaning into him for support. She felt so lightheaded it was as if she were weightless. His mouth was moving over her face and neck… He bent her backwards, kissing the shadowed cleft between her breasts.

Desire welled up as if from a gushing spring. "You hurt me badly."

"You hurt *me*."

"It still matters, Ashe," she gasped, hollow with yearning.

"Of course it does." The pads of his thumbs were working her erect nipples.

Reason was obliterated. She closed her eyes the better to lock in the ecstasy. No one had ever made love to her like Ashe. His hand was on the zipper of her dress. He pulled it down and the silken fold of fabric fell away from her, sliding to her feet. She stood in her undergarments. "I want you so badly," he said in such a quiet voice, it was barely a breath. "Don't fight me on this, Cate." His hands covered the slopes of her warm, smooth breasts.

I'm going to die of longing, she thought. Only just coping, she eased herself into him, her flesh melting like candle wax. "One last time?"

"And the one after, and the one after that…"

He lifted her slowly, easily, carrying her into the bedroom and laying her down on the king-sized bed. "You never know, you might like it. You certainly used to."

They were staring into one another's eyes, each seeking their own reflection. "It was different back then. I'm not the same. I was young."

His laugh was gently mocking. "You're the same." He passed a masterly hand over her body. It visibly quivered at his touch, awaiting further excitation. She was lying prone on the bed, her long legs extended, yet she felt as though he were drawing her up. "People change, but what we had lasts. I called it love. God knows what you called it, but you want me just as much as I want you." He lowered himself onto the side of the bed studying her, so beautiful, so womanly, so made for loving. "Go on, deny it. If you can." He began to caress her, his hand moving slowly over her, his palms against her flesh, her breasts, her stomach, his fingers sliding below the line of her briefs moving downwards, pressing, sending fiery sensations shooting through her. The sense of excitement, of utter intoxication, was extreme; the bursts of pleasure were such she thought she would come to a shuddering climax merely from the rotating movements of his long, caressing fingers.

That harsh breathing she suddenly realised was hers. She sounded very agitated. God, how she needed this! Her whole body was flowering, opening up to him. The needs of her body were in total control now. Her skin glittered with a faint dew as pressure built. She felt a crazed desperation to have him inside her.

"Ashe," she moaned like a woman only just holding it together. "Make love to me." Far, far

into the night. At the same time what remained of cold reason told her:

He planned this. Planned it perfectly.

And you went along with it. Why?

She knew why. She was worn down by the years of intense loneliness, of the sense of deprivation, for that was what it had been without Ashe. Without love. Sex was a crucial part of it, but what they'd had had been more noble, engaging both mind and spirit. Still the lack of sex in the way she wanted it had weighed on her heavily. Now the drive towards fulfilment was gaining irresistible momentum.

She didn't realise it but tears were rolling down her cheeks. He bent his dark head, catching them up with his mouth as though each teardrop were as precious as a flawless diamond...

Naked, her skin gleamed like satin in the soft light. He had turned away swiftly to strip off his clothes, not bothering to hang them over anything, but discarding them where they fell. She called his name, begging him not to delay. She was desperate to merge her body with his.

It had been so long. So long. No one before or after her. She was his woman, first and last. Rockhard, Ashe moved towards the bed.

Their destinies were entwined.

He had found her. He had found his son.

They were his. He would never let them go. This

was the most important mission of his life. His objective was to win. Nothing was as important to him as Catrina and Julian. They were his family.

He came to her, whispering into her open mouth, "Thy fate and mine are sealed."

CHAPTER NINE

CATE AND STELLA rarely had disagreements. They dealt calmly and considerately with one another and they had Jules in common. But when Cate arrived home much later than expected, Stella had the attitude of a woman on the warpath. Obviously there was some undisclosed crisis going on in her mind.

"Nearly twelve o'clock, right?"

"Hey, you gave me a fright." Cate actually jumped. Stella was standing right inside the front door. Her expression made Cate feel like a problematic teenager home much too late. "I didn't know I had to clock in and out." Cate tried a joke. "What's the problem?"

Stella's dark eyes were deeply shadowed. "We both know what the problem is," she said severely, as though Cate's past were being reactivated. "It's Julian Carlisle. He broke your heart once. Are you going to allow him to do it again?"

Cate groaned. "Stella, do you really want to get into this now?"

"Answer me." Stella spoke as if she had the right.

"With respect, I think that might be my business."

Stella wasn't about to apologise. "He wants Jules. You know that. He'll stop at nothing to get him. Jules, *my* Jules. *My* family."

Cate put her bag down, counting to ten. "Stella can we have this conversation at another time? I want to go to bed."

"But you've been to bed, haven't you?" Stella accused. Strong emotion was swirling at the backs of her eyes. "You have the look of a woman who's been very thoroughly bedded." Concrete evidence Cate had no moral strength. Like Annabel perhaps?

Cate shook her head. "I don't believe I'm hearing this, Stella. What I do is my business, not yours."

But Stella was on a roll, challenging as she had never been before. "It's clear to me you have no will of your own when he's around. You know how hard it's been getting over him. Now, you're back in the firing line."

Cate was dismayed and confused. Was this the Stella she had lived with all her life or a far more aggressive twin? "Stella, I'm not talking about this now," she said carefully. "You didn't have to wait up for me. I'm a grown woman. Not in *your* firing line. You're actually overstepping the mark."

"Am I now?" Stella gave a harsh laugh. "I certainly *did* have to wait up for you. I'm very worried about you, Catrina." She thrust her hair behind one ear.

"Well, you don't have to be." Cate backed away.

"I don't believe that," Stella hit back. "You should see yourself!'

To Cate's stunned ears it had a ring of *jealousy*. Was that possible? Stella was jealous of her? It seemed preposterous. Yet if it were so, she didn't know how to deal with it. She turned to look in the tall gilt-framed mirror over the hallway console. She did look different. She looked blazingly *alive*, an erotic creature still wearing the veils of ecstasy. "I look fine, though my hair is a bit on the messy side." Unlike its usual order, her hair tumbled in a thick golden mane. Even she knew she looked beautiful. What did Stella see?

Stella saw something she didn't like because her face was a set mask. "I hope you took precautions?" she said severely, as though endlessly plagued by concerns in this regard. "We don't want a repeat of the last time."

"The last time?" This from kind-hearted Stella? Cate forced calm on herself.

"Like mother, like daughter," Stella affirmed wringing her hands like a latter-day Lady Macbeth

"Now that's uncalled for, Stella." Cate suddenly exploded. "It would be very unwise of us to continue this conversation."

But Stella, for the first time in living memory was stripped of her calm façade. "No matter how clever you are, you're not ahead of the game," she said, just short of contempt. "You're still liable to make mistakes."

Cate's stomach was lurching sickly. "I though we all were. *You're* making a mistake right now This is *my* home, Stella, might I remind you. *I* pay the mortgage. You held on to your assets, which we both know are considerable. We've been very happy here. What's all this about anyway? You're saying I'm like Annabel, your *alleged* beloved little sister, maybe not so beloved after all?"

Stella's dark eyes glittered with intensity. This was a Stella from another world, another time "Both of you brought a mess on yourselves and had to deal with it. Beguiling little Annabel and her legions of lovers!" she exclaimed bitterly. "She didn't know about gentleness, tenderness, care. All she knew was running wild!"

"How dare you?" Cate found herself ready and willing to spring to her mother's defence. "Listen to the way you're talking. It's disgusting You're talking about your dead sister and to *me* her daughter. It's far more likely Annabel was a fascinating woman. That's why she had so many admirers. It's even possible you've totally misrepresented her. I see that now. You made confidences to people about your sister and people listened. You told me yourself you were much admired for your utter selflessness."

"I loved her," Stella continued as though she hadn't heard a word Cate said. "But I loved Ralph more. The tragedy was he didn't see me with Annabel around. It made no sense. Annabel wasn't anywhere near as stable as I. But men were like moths to the flame with her. Most people thought I was the nicer person and just as good-looking. Only I lacked the *look after me* image. It worked brilliantly for Annabel. I was the unselfish one who coped and endured."

"Here is a woman who has eaten the bread of righteousness," Cate quoted bleakly. "I hear what you say, Stella, now I'm making a belated assessment. You were *hugely* jealous of Annabel."

"Nonsense!"

Cate continued unimpressed. "You envied the excitement, the allure, that rippled around her. She couldn't help it. She was born that way. Please don't erode the love I have left for you, Stella. Say no more. Go to bed. Sleep on it."

"To be perfectly honest—"

"Have you ever been perfectly honest?" A hard

core of grief and disillusionment was in Cate's voice.

"I've never felt better." Stella straightened her shoulders like a woman with a long list of good deeds behind her. "Seeing Julian Carlisle, now the two of you together, has brought it all back."

"What does it bring back, Stella?" Cate asked, moving into the living room. It was a precaution. Jules was a deep sleeper, but there was a possibility he could wake up at the sound of their voices. "You're saying you loved Rafe Stewart?" She had to press Stella into answering now. Stella might have the dubious gift of being able to wipe things from her mind, but *she* couldn't. She had to *know*.

"Stop being such a complete idiot! Of course I did. I was mad about him. He was the most wonderful catch. He was attracted to me *first*, I was thrilled, but Annabel went after him. She felt no shame. She really needed to do penance."

Cate felt as if she had been pitched head first into hell. "What, *die*?" she exploded. "Annabel, my mother, deserved to die? And die relatively young? Are you saying all your years of self-sacrifice were no more than a cover-up orchestrated by you? I knew you didn't love Arnold. Poor old Arnold knew it too. He knew he was second best. You loved someone else. Did you marry Arnold on the rebound? To save face. You couldn't have Rafe, but eventually you learned you could have his child. *Me.* Is that it? Rafe Stewart is my father?" She drew closer to Stella, her voice soaring despite her efforts at restraint.

Jules woke with a fright. He sat up in bed, blinking his eyes. He could hear voices coming from downstairs. His mother and his grandmother were having an argument. It didn't seem possible. They all loved one another. Something was wrong. Immediately he resolved to get up. He had to go and check. He often thought of himself as a soldier, a brave soldier, a fighting man, going into battle. He would fight to the death for his mother. And Nan too, of course. But his mother was the most important person in the world to him.

He tripped over a rug, muttered a little swear word he wasn't supposed to say—all the kids did—then opened the door of his bedroom. He had left it ajar because he knew his mother always liked to kiss him goodnight. Most of the time he waited for it. But tonight he had fallen asleep. Out in the hallway the voices were louder. He moved very quietly to the top of the stairs, a lone little figure in pyjamas.

They *were* arguing. Just to know that was akin to what he thought an electric shock might be like. Nan was speaking in a voice he had never heard before. Or ever suspected she had. It was a voice that frightened him. Nan sounded as if she no longer loved his mother. She sounded as if she had been cheated in some way. Not by his mother, never!

Oh, please don't let this happen!

I must stop it.

For some reason not at all clear to him a vivid picture of Lord Wyndham sprang into his mind. Lord Wyndham was a man of authority. Moreover, he was a relative of Nan's, which meant there was an extended family connection to all of them. Lord Wyndham could help.

Nan's new-sounding voice hung in the air. "When are you going to tell the boy Carlisle is his father?" she asked tersely.

That came like a great clap of thunder. Stunned, Jules jerked to one side, in case he be obliterated by a bolt of lightning.

"I must tell him. I will tell him." His mother sounded tremendously upset. Her upset was transferring itself to him, forcing him to his knees. It was Nan who was going out on the attack. His mother was on the receiving end. He couldn't let that happen. The Jules he was, Jules Hamilton, had suddenly ceased to be. He was Jules Somebody Else. Why hadn't he put it all together? He was supposed to be smart. He wasn't smart at all. He was just a dumb kid who had lost all his powers.

Carlisle! That means Lord Wyndham is your father.

But his father had deserted his mother and him years ago. Jules felt as if he were drowning. Not that he *could* drown. He was a very good swimmer. But his legs suddenly felt so weak he sank onto the top step, his head in his hands. Now he was unashamedly listening. This was all about him, his mother and Lord Wyndham, who had never been there for them.

"He'd love that, wouldn't he?" Nan sounded close to snarling. Not like Nan at all. "He's always wanted a father."

"Why wouldn't he?" his mother broke in. "Everyone wants a father, a loving father. You've always told me Annabel refused to name my father, even on her deathbed, but you've always known, haven't you, Stella? You've always known I'm Rafe Stewart's daughter. I was supposed to be the 'little cross' you took on. But you were actually *glad* to take me on, weren't you, Stella? You couldn't have him, but you had his child. You triumphed over Annabel there."

Jules found himself gasping for breath. What was happening here? He could almost wish he had stayed asleep.

"Do I detect a note of daughterly love?" Stella sounded scoffing. "You've always been so down on *Aunt* Annabel."

"How did you convince her to give me up?" It seemed to Jules there were tears in his mother's voice. His mother never cried. Not in front of him anyway. His mother was his life.

"It was easy," Nan said. "My influence over Annabel began when we were only small children. Our parents had one another. They didn't need us, especially after the Big Tragedy. You know, losing the heir. I convinced Annabel she was doing the right thing. She knew poor old Arnie and I would take the greatest care of you."

"Did Arnold know about Rafe?" his mother asked.

Rafe? Who was Rafe? Jules was struggling to understand but he couldn't take it all in.

"He may have guessed," Nan was saying. "He never knew. I certainly wasn't about to tell him."

His mother, who always sounded so bright and confident, now sounded deeply distressed. "Who the hell are you, Stella? How do I deal with the *two* of you? Stella One has been very good to me and to Jules. I thank her for that. But Stella Two, your alternate persona, is a formidable woman. I see how you built your life and my life on a pack of lies."

Nan's *new* voice burst out. "We could have gone on as before, *for ever*, if need be. The three of us, if only Carlisle hadn't come back into your life. And of course you still love him. How pathetic! So what does he want to do—take you both back to England? Don't think for a second he'll marry you. He didn't before."

Oh, Mummy, oh, Mummy. Jules wobbled to his feet. This wasn't fair. Nan didn't sound kind. She sounded cruel. It was important he be there for his mother.

"You're not the only designing woman in my life, Stella," his mother was saying. "You and Alicia Carlisle would have made a good match. I don't know which of you has done the greatest damage. I don't want to hear one more word from you. I'm going up to bed. We can't go on like this, Stella. You realise that. Not after all you've said."

There was the sound of high heels on the polished floor. His mother was coming upstairs.

"I love you, Catrina. I love Jules." Nan was calling to his mother in a hollow voice.

"What price love?" his mother answered.

Jules didn't know what to do. In a few moments his mother would reach the landing. He needed to talk to someone. He turned about, making a rush for the shelter of his bedroom. He knew he couldn't possibly sleep. Not after all he had heard. His head was still ringing with the sound of Nan's angry voice. Jules leapt into bed, pulling the light coverlet over him. He turned his face to the wall. He felt like crying, but dragged himself out of it. Soldiers didn't cry.

A few moments later he felt his mother's light kiss on his cheek.

"Goodnight, my darling," she said.

Goodnight, Mummy.

Your enemies are my enemies.

He spoke silently. He couldn't find a voice to answer her. He pretended to be sound asleep. It was what she would have wanted anyway. He knew perfectly well his mother would be tremendously upset to know he had overheard her argument with Nan.

Only she's not your nan, is she?

You have a father. You have a mother AND a father. Only your father denied you your birthright.

For a moment seven-year-old Jules was gripped by near-adult fury. *Why* had his father abandoned him and his mother? What his mother had told him wasn't good enough. He determined he would find out the real reason. He would have it out with this man, his father, Lord Wyndham. He didn't care if he was a lord or not. Titles had nothing to do with anything so far as he was concerned.

He would have it out with Mr Wyndham the very next day. The insult was so great.

You need to give me some answers. I'm nearly eight years old. I have a right to express my feelings.

Yet his beautiful mother—the most beautiful mother in the world—abandoned or not, had named him after his father. *Julian*. Why would she do that? Nothing made sense. Yet he knew what he had to do. He had to protect her.

Jules' heart was racing. He was in a bit of a panic. He waited until his mother drove away before he crossed to the other side of the road, pretending he was waiting for a school friend. The seconds seemed to be spinning into hours. As usual there were so many cars dropping off kids. He hoped Noah's mum would be late this morning. He didn't want to have to confront Noah. He was a man on a mission. It was a hot morning so he wasn't wearing Kingsley's distinctive school blazer. He should have had his hat on, but he didn't. His heart was now up in his throat. Sooner or later some conscientious mother was bound to ask him what he was doing. His mother always checked up on stray kids.

Like a miracle, a taxi double parked for a moment right in front of him. One of the older boys got out, slamming the door. "What are you up to, Hamilton?" He fixed his eyes on the younger boy.

Jules saw a heaven-sent opportunity. "Hi, Daniel. I have to go back into town. I have a dentist appointment Mum forgot. My nan is going to take me." He appealed to the taxi driver. "Can you drive me back to the city, please? I have to meet my nan outside the Four Seasons Hotel. I have the money."

The taxi driver shouldn't have, but he said, "Right-o, hop in."

"I hope you're telling the truth, Hamilton?" the older boy asked, clearly dissatisfied with Jules' story.

"Please, don't hold us up, Daniel. I won't make it on time."

"All right, go, then," Daniel said. "But I'm going to check with your teacher," he warned.

"That's okay!" Jules waved a hand. "See you later."

"Playing the wag, are you?" the taxi driver, a jovial man, asked when they were under way.

"No, no! I need to get to the hotel. Please hurry."

"Better to keep to the speed limit," his driver chortled. The boy looked like an angel. Clearly he was not.

Safely inside the hotel, Jules marched straight up to Reception. For a minute or two the smart young woman behind the reception desk ignored him. "What are you doing here, little boy? Shouldn't you be at school?"

"I'm here to see Lord Wyndham," Jules answered, slightly intimidated despite himself.

The receptionist actually laughed. "Are you just! And who shall I say is calling?"

"Please tell him it's Jules," he said, squaring his shoulders. She needed to take him seriously.

"Jules who?" The receptionist placed the boy's age at around seven. He was a very handsome boy with thick blond hair and beautiful sapphire-blue eyes. His accent sounded English to her ears. He seemed excessively precocious for a kid his age. He really needed a set-down.

"Lord Wyndham knows me," Jules said without a blink. "I'm a relative of his." He formulated the words clearly.

"Of course you are!" the receptionist cried with splendid disbelief. Here was a kid of seven, going on seventy.

"May I speak to the manager?" Jules was eager to confront his father. He remembered his mother had asked to speak to the manager once when they were in Hong Kong. "If you could find him for me?" he suggested politely. "Or you could ring Lord Wyndham and check with him."

The receptionist's indignation became evident. She was seriously taken aback. Who did this kid think he was? "A great favourite of his, are you?"

"I did say I'm a relative," Jules reminded her.

The receptionist physically jerked back. "One minute," she said crisply. "You'll be in big trouble, sonny, if you're playing some sort of game. Sit down over there in the lobby." She pointed an officious hand.

"Thank you so much," said Jules, ever polite.

The receptionist's smile had a vague air of malevolence.

What a kid! Anyone would think he was royalty! The receptionist, huffing to herself, put through the call to Lord Wyndham's suite. There was probably one chance in a million the drop-dead gorgeous Wyndham knew the boy. The kid was most likely up to some prank. But she had to hand it to him. He had *style*.

To her astonishment, when she told Lord Wyndham a boy called Jules was waiting for him in the lobby he told her he would be right down.

How about that? She could have short-circuited her career in hotel management. Come to think of it the boy had Lord Wyndham's amazingly blue eyes and thick black lashes. He could very well be a relative.

She waited until Lord Wyndham walked into the lobby. She saw the tall, handsome British lord put his hand on the boy's shoulder, probably asking him what he was there for. The boy's face was upturned to him. He was speaking earnestly, with the look of someone who had a perfect right to be there. The next thing the two of them walked off towards the bank of lifts.

I ask you! Quite obviously the boy wasn't just any kid. He had identified himself as "Jules". Lord Wyndham had booked in as Julian Carlisle. She mulled over that nugget of information, wondering if it would be useful.

Cate was at her desk, when Stella rang. "What is it, Stella?" she asked, still not over her terrible upset at her aunt's behaviour. "I'm busy at the moment."

Stella lost no time relaying the news the school had rung. Jules had not turned up. He wasn't in class. An older boy Daniel Morris had spoken to him before school. Jules claimed he had to go into the city for a dentist appointment his mother had forgotten. He was to meet his grandmother. Jules got into the same cab the older boy had taken to school and told the cab driver he was meeting his grandmother at the Four Seasons Hotel.

The Four Seasons Hotel? Jules had gone to where Ashe was staying.

She was about to hang up on Stella, telling her she would handle it, only Stella chipped in, "He's gone to his father," she said. "His *father*, over *you*. Over *me*. He won't want us now."

Realisation dawned on Cate. Stella felt threatened, whereas she didn't feel threatened at all. She had come to see she had been given a chance in a million. The chance to put things right. Fate had brought her and Ashe together again despite the forces that had been at work against them. They would now have to work out the future. Right now, she had to ring the school, and then get herself to the Four Seasons Hotel. At that moment her job meant little to her. She had worked so hard, worked endless hours, all night sometimes. What did it add up to? She had known for years she was missing out on *real* life. She could no longer deny Ashe had a right to be part of his son's life. There were hard decisions to be made.

By the time Ashe made his phone call to Catrina—he had listened in silence to his son's impassioned stream of questions, before answering them as quietly and seriously as he knew how—he was told she had left work citing a family emergency. He swiftly put two and two together. She was coming to the hotel. Jules had told him all about the taxi ride into town. He walked away from the child into the other room to ring Stella. Jules had told him as well about "the fight" and the revelations that had emerged. For some reason Ashe realised he had queered his pitch with Stella, his kinswoman. This was instantly confirmed from the coldness of Stella's voice. Nevertheless he went on to assure her Jules was safe with him.

"Think you can show up when you like!" Her voice was startlingly loud in his ear.

"When and where I like, Stella," he said, dismayed by her reaction. "I'm paying you the courtesy of telling you my son and your great-nephew is safe."

"You want to know a secret?" Stella's icy voice came back at him in retaliation. "She's Rafe Stewart's daughter."

"Just as I thought." Ashe's reply was remarkably calm. "Does that set your conscience free, Stella? I should have recognised that wonderful colouring, the gold and the green. But you knew all along, didn't you? To think how you've deceived your own niece!"

"How could I not?" the gentle, unflappable Stella returned vehemently.

"That's not love," Ashe lamented. "You were driven by some form of *hate*."

"She was born looking so like him." Stella sounded as though she was talking more to herself than to him.

"The young man who was madly in love with Annabel, not you," Ashe said quietly. "I don't like to dwell on how you went about damaging Annabel's reputation. You were very cunning. You had to diminish her in people's eyes. Sadly you were often believed. Even I heard the stories of wicked little Annabel Radclyffe. Poor misjudged Annabel, I'd now say. Goodbye, Stella. I believe Catrina is on her way here. Her father, Rafe Stewart, will be thrilled out of his mind to finally meet her."

"Don't count on it!" Stella made a harsh grunting noise.

"I am counting on it. Rafe will know who she

is before ever a word is spoken. You force-fed Ca
trina a pack of lies." His tone told her plainly she
had acted very badly.

"I have a special gift for them," Stella retorted
unfazed. Then, to his dismay, laughed. "We go
on well without you. And Rafe," she said. "Now
you've got the lot!"

"What goes around, comes around, Stella," was
his reply.

When a knock came, Jules rushed to the door
"That will be Mummy," he cried excitedly.

"Well, let her in, Julian," Ashe advised calmly
He was still recovering from being taken to task
with a vengeance by a small boy who just hap
pened to be his son. He couldn't think of a single
soul who had confronted him thus unless it was
Jules' mother. It was made very clear to him pro
tecting his mother was central to Jules' existence
He, the father, was perceived as the man who had
disavowed them. That was his son's world as i
was and as he saw it. He had used all his pow
ers of persuasion to get the boy to sit down so
they could talk it out, even to the extent of getting
into human relationships and moral issues. He had
pointed out Jules would find as an adult there were
always harsh realities in life to confront. He had
set out his case. He had left it to Jules to deter
mine the outcome. It was tremendously importan

for his son to understand the circumstances that had driven him and Catrina apart. He thought he might have been pushing a seven-year-old boy to his extreme limits but his son's high intelligence was well on display. Catrina had reared their son well. She had given him a childhood of stability and love. Jules was a confident child. For one so young he had achieved an impressive state of equilibrium. The silent rages that he had quite naturally harboured against his missing father had been at long last addressed. Hopefully the scars would fade.

His son's question gave him the answer. "Is everything going to be all right?" It was clear he had become an authority figure.

"Of course it is, Julian. Open the door," Ashe bid him calmly.

Mother and son fell into one another's arms. "Don't you ever do that again!" Cate cried, bending over her precious child. "Not *ever*!" she repeated fiercely, her eyes moving over Jules' blond head to find Ashe. Ashe nodded to her, knowing she was reading his mind. Their son's issues had been addressed. "Why didn't you speak to me, Jules?" Cate turned back to her son. "You should have spoken to me."

He had already been told that by his father. Still, he spoke his mind. "I had to handle this myself."

His blue eyes were very bright. "But I'm very sorry, Mum, if you were worried."

"Worried!" Cate echoed, casting her eyes up to heaven.

"All's well that ends well." Ashe spoke gently from behind them. "Come in, Catrina. Shut the door. You've rung the school?"

"Of course." She looked into his face, all her old love for him surging back. One could live a lifetime and still not know the evils that existed inside other people's souls. Jealousy was a deadly sin. The people that were closest to them—for Ashe, his mother; for her, her aunt Stella—had caused so much damage it was a miracle they had finally won through. It was their job now to refocus on the future and what was best for their son. Ashe wanted him. He wanted her. Past history would not be allowed to tarnish the future.

"You'll be in a spot of bother at school, Julian," Ashe was telling his son.

"What can they do to me?" Jules kept his arm around his mother, feeling a great upsurge of happiness, of *family*. "They wouldn't expel me, would they?"

"No, but you won't get off scot-free." Ashe made it perfectly clear. "You may have thought you were doing the right thing, but you weren't. There was your mother to be considered, and others. The school has a duty of care. It's a very serious matter when a child takes it into their head to go AWOL."

"I know what that means," said Jules. "Away without leave?"

"It does." Ashe nodded. His son had confided he liked to think of himself as a soldier. No bad thing at all.

"It was a blessing Daniel told your teacher." Cate sighed in relief.

Jules pulled a wry face. "I knew he would. He suspected I wasn't telling the truth, anyway."

"Your taxi driver has a problem." Cate was reminded. "He shouldn't have taken you on as a passenger."

"I think he thought it was a joke." Jules tried to get the jovial taxi driver off the hook. "So did the receptionist downstairs. She thought I was having her on."

"Regardless, there are rules to be obeyed, Julian," Ashe said firmly. "Rules of good behaviour have to pertain."

"Yes, sir." Jules dipped his head respectfully. "Do I have to go back to school today?" he asked, looking from one to the other, hoping they would say no.

"Yes, you do," Ashe said, putting an end to his son's speculation. "We'll go with you. But you have to make your own apologies. No excuses."

"I can do that," Jules said, cheering up enormously. They were going together. He, his mother and now his *father*! It was wonderful, *wonderful*, knowing his father wanted him. His father had confided the whole story to him, man to man. His father had told him his mother, Catrina, was the great love of his life.

That made two of them.

He watched while his mother walked into his father's outstretched arms. He watched his father bend his dark head to kiss her, a really super-duper kiss, just like the movies. He didn't mind in the least. Mothers and fathers were supposed to kiss one another.

"I expect I'll enjoy Christmas in England," he suddenly announced to his startled parents. "I know so many carols. And there could be *snow*! Wouldn't that be wonderful, Mum?"

His mother's beautiful smile quivered. "Wonderful, Jules!" she seconded.

"Right!" His father stretched out an imperious hand. "Time to go back to school, Julian, and face the music."

"Okay. I know I've done wrong." Jules held out both his hands. "Can I tell the kids my dad has come for me? Can I?"

"I don't see why not," Cate said, lacing her fingers through his, while his father took his other hand.

"I know 'Stille Nacht, Heilige Nacht' in German," Jules told his father proudly. "I really would love to be able to speak several languages. You told me my grandfather, my *real* grandfather, could."

"Then you've got a head start," said Lord Julian Wyndham. "I can help you. I speak a couple myself."

"Maybe we can take Nan too," Jules said. "Back to England, I mean, for the trip. I'm sure she'll apologise for getting so angry. I expect she was worried."

It was obvious to them both Jules was waiting for their answer.

"We'll see," said his mother. "Now, best get going."

"Face the music," said Jules, a bounce in his step. He had fantasised about having a great dad. A great dad would have made his world complete.

Now he had one.

CHAPTER TEN

Christmas.
Radclyffe Hall.
England.

JULES CROSSED THE great hall of this wonderful old house where Nan had been born. Why hadn't anyone told him? Adults seemed to keep so much to themselves. He didn't know why and he wouldn't know for a long time. But when he'd first caught sight of the beautiful old manor house set high on the hill he had burst out, "Things like this only happen in fairy tales, don't they, Mum?" The sight had enchanted him.

She had ruffled his hair and given him the loveliest smile. "Actually they happen more often than we think, my darling." He had never seen his mother look more beautiful or more happy. She even called him Julian now and then and he pretended not to notice. Anyway, he didn't mind. Julian seemed to suit him better here in England.

He loved England. He thought London was a splendid city with so many monuments and so much history. He had stood in awe outside Buckingham Palace where the Queen lived. The Queen was still Queen of Australia. He was loving everything, but he missed home and he missed his friends, particularly Noah. Radclyffe Hall and the beautiful countryside were special but it did rain a lot and it was very *cold*. He had never been so cold in his life, even with lots of warm clothes on, a beanie pulled down over his forehead and over his ears. Woollen mittens. Now that wasn't *cool*. The cold wrapped around him but he was starting to get a bit used to it. Acclimatisation they called it. He didn't know if it would ever happen though. He loved the *sun*.

He missed Nan too, but she had decided to stay at home. Before they'd left she had told his mother she was giving a good deal of thought to marrying their family solicitor, Gerald Enright. He didn't have a clue why she would want to marry Mr Enright—he was a nice man but quite old—but his mother said they would suit very well.

He pushed open the heavy door of what his father called the Yellow Drawing Room, with a feeling of glorious anticipation, shutting it quietly behind him. It was early morning. No one had spotted him as he had come down the stairs, though he had heard brisk footsteps from somewhere at the rear of the grand house. A row of luxury cars stood at the front of the house in the huge circular drive with all the pudding-shaped bushes his father told him were yews. He had studied with interest the Bentleys, the Rolls and two Mercedes. It was cold enough for snow to fall, he thought, but the longed-for snow hadn't fallen as yet. He knew it would. He was so looking forward to it.

Passing under the great chandeliers, Jules crossed the beautiful, big room to where the great Christmas tree glittered and shone. His mother and his aunt Olivia had decorated it with a delirium of fantastically beautiful and plentiful baubles—gorgeous jewelled butterflies Aunty Olivia had taken out of storage for this year's festivities. Many of the ornaments were very old, handed down through the generations. So the tree looked absolutely splendid, even more so at night when all the dazzling fairy lights were turned on. His mother and Aunt Olivia had had to stand on ladders to decorate the higher branches.

Around the base of the tree were swags and swags of presents wrapped up in sumptuous papers and embellished with ribbons. Silver-sprayed bare branches in tall blue and white Chinese pots stood over at the long windows. Bronze deers had been placed beside them. Garlands of silver and scarlet flowers, with lots of greenery in between and lovely little ornaments that included white

doves, were strung along the chimney piece of
the white marble fireplace. They had all worked
hard to make it happen. Even the banisters of the
great staircase had been decorated with hanging
bunches of green foliage and big red baubles tied
with silver, gold and scarlet ribbon. He thought
he would carry a vivid memory of that Christmas
tree, the first he would see at Radclyffe Hall, for
the rest of his life.

Aunt Olivia had a son, Peter, a bit younger than
he. They were cousins. Fancy that! Already they
got on well. In fact, they had accepted one another right off. He and Peter had been allowed to
help. Afterwards, his father had taken him upon
his shoulders to place the Christmas angel at the
top of the tree. Everyone had clapped, making his
heart swell with happiness. He started to think of
all the generations of his family, the Radclyffes,
who had looked on the Christmas tree with awe.
Years after he would be told the whole story. But
this was *now*.

Aunt Leonie and her family would be arriving
this morning. Other relatives had already arrived.
They were house guests in a home that had so
many bedrooms it could have been a small hotel.
It was going to be one "splendid do!" said one of
his father's guests, a lovely man, called Mr Stewart, who was a famous politician. He was so looking forward to the two of them having a talk. Mr

Stewart had promised. Of course he had already confided to Mr Stewart he wanted to be a politician too. In fact, Prime Minister of Australia was his long-term goal.

"So you've made up your mind?" Mr Stewart had asked with such kindness and keen interest in his face.

"Yes, sir."

"Then you have a goal, Julian?"

"Yes, I do, sir. I want to live a life that has meaning."

For a moment Mr Stewart looked startled, then he stared right into the small boy's eyes, blue like a gas flame. Carlisle eyes. "There's wisdom deep inside you, Julian. We need men and women of wisdom. Stick with your goal."

"I will, sir." Jules was thrilled by Mr Stewart's words of encouragement. Mr Stewart was a great man.

"And I'll be following your progress closely." Mr Stewart had clasped his shoulder as if he meant to be a part of his life. When they had first met, Mrs Stewart had bent to kiss his face. She was a lovely lady with soft, gentle, haunted eyes that made him want to comfort her. He knew now just being an adult there could be sad, scary times. He had already seen most people's lives weren't without sadness. His mother had been sad for a long time. Yet she had always said, "We have to find a quiet place to nurture the spirit, Jules. Try our hardest to be positive."

He thought so too. What he didn't realise was it was quite an insight for a boy of seven going on eight. Jules had in fact made a profound impact on everybody. Aunt Olivia had hugged him and hugged him, crooning, *"Julian, Julian,"* over and over, cradling his head. When she had kissed him there were tears in her eyes. Everyone seemed to really like him. And he liked them. It gave him a wonderful feeling, like opening a window on the magical power of belonging. It was going to be the best Christmas of his life. He hoped everyone would sing in church. He had been practising his carols. He knew they were all going to the village church later on in the morning. He believed people should pray. There was no need to bottle up all one's troubles. Tell God and He would listen. Hadn't He listened to him?

Christmas Day went off splendidly. Cate and Olivia had consulted with Cook to come up with a mouth-watering menu. There were entrées and main courses. Roast turkey and roast goose. Jules had never tried that one before, but he liked it. Plenty of yummy desserts, including little meringue snowmen, jolly little fellows, their hats made out of black decorating icing, black button eyes, an upturned red mouth and down the front of the snowman's chest, a red scarf. Cook had made them especially for the children. They were a big hit. There was Christmas pudding, of course, that was brought flaming to the table. It was all so different from Christmas at home where the sun blazed and everyone ate lots of seafood, prawns, crabs with lovely, fresh white meat, lobster and large platters of different salads. Afterwards, when the meal settled they all headed off for the beach and a cooling swim.

There was a lovely warmth around the gleaming dining-room table with its decorative swag running its full length of the centre. The table was so long there was plenty of room for everyone to spread out. The joy of it all had caught Jules a bit by surprise. His father's family and his father's extended family had welcomed him and his mother, tucking them neatly and lovingly into the fold. It seemed to him that was what Christmas was all about.

It was Mr Stewart who put word to it. "'Remembrance, like a candle, burns brightest at Christmastime.'"

Everyone had clapped and Mr Stewart had said with a laugh, "I can't take the credit. That lies with a Mr Charles Dickens."

Much later that night, when the entire household had long since retired, Catrina and Ashe lay together in his great warm bed, their bodies spooned into one another. Ashe had his arms around the woman he loved, the woman he had lost, the woman he had regained, the mother of his son. He could feel every bone in her slender body; his hand cupped her small, perfect breast like a creamy-white rosebud unfurled. He adored her.

"What are you thinking?" he murmured into her ear.

"How happy I am." She gave a voluptuous sigh, turning on her back to face him, looking up into his bluer than blue eyes. "Safe, secure, loved. As a family we're united. What more could I want?"

He bent and languidly, but very sensually, kissed her mouth. "I can't make Jules into a little Pom."

They both laughed. Recognition of that fact had set him back, but he was admiring of his son's firm mindset even at age seven. Julian was having a wonderful time but it was clear after the long vacation was over in early February he wanted to go home.

Home was Australia. Ashe had the definite notion his son thought he, as his father, would take charge of the whole situation and find a solution.

"He wants to go home, Ashe," Cate said, as if he needed any reminder. "He's loving it here, but he calls Australia home. So do I." She placed her hands against his chest, her tapering fingers tangling in his light chest hair.

"So it's up to me." It wasn't a question.

"Darling, I'm not saying that. I'm—"

"You *are*." He kissed her again. "You're so beautiful. Naked you look like a mermaid with your green eyes and long, golden hair. Rafe is thrilled out of his mind. He told me over and over he thinks Jules is an amazing little fellow. So does dear Helena. What makes Rafe happy makes Helena happy. They're in your life now, my love."

"I know and I feel blessed." Cate meant it. "Everyone has been so beautiful to me."

"That's because *you're* beautiful." He smoothed her tumbled hair from her forehead, pressing her back into the pillows. "Julian told me he loves to draw you because you're so beautiful."

Tears swam into Cate's eyes. Jules had told her that too.

"And you're going to make an exquisite bride," said Jules' father. The two of them had agreed on an April wedding at Radclyffe Hall. Beyond that, they were still trying to work out what was best for them as a family. Wherever Ashe was, Cate would go. Ashe was her world. Only he wasn't her *entire* world. There was their son. Many of her hopes could well be sunk, but she realised neither of them was prepared to destabilise Jules. After all, he was a young man with big plans.

"How mysterious is the way destiny works." Ashe kissed her open mouth, breathing in her sweet breath. "I intend to have a word with Liv and Bram in the morning," he said, as though he had finally reached a mulled-over decision.

"What about?" Cate's green eyes, which had been shut in rapture, snapped open.

"We're looking for a solution, aren't we? We could have one if Liv and Bram agree."

Cate sat up in bed, not bothering to pull the sheet over her naked body. Ashe knew every inch of her. "You have a plan?"

"Do I?" He lay back, pulling her down over the top of him. One arm locked around her back. "Well, it's a practical solution until Jules is much older and better able perhaps to make up his mind. I'm going to offer the house and the running of the estate to Liv and Bram. They absolutely love it here—always have—and Peter can go to the excellent village school until he's ready to be sent to whatever school they choose. They will act as custodians. I want nothing from them. They will live rent free. Bram will get paid as the manager of the estate. It's a suggestion I'm going to put to them."

Cate was too close to tears to speak. "You mean you're prepared to come and live in Australia?" she asked, as if a great blessing had descended on her. "But what about all you have *here*, to say nothing of your business interests?"

"My darling Cate, don't worry. Clever business-woman that you are, you know business can be conducted from virtually anywhere. Besides, I like Australia. I like the people. You and Julian especially. Sydney is a beautiful and liveable city. I can't say I won't have to make a lot of trips around the globe. I will. I need to oversee my interests which I remind you will become yours. I want you on board, not only as my wife, but as my business partner. Your input would be much appreciated."

She felt such a degree of relief she nearly shouted aloud with joy. "I don't know what to say, Ashe."

"Say, what a wonderful solution." He afforded her his beautiful smile.

"It's a *marvellous* solution, providing you're absolutely sure?"

"I'm absolutely sure I want you and our son in my life. Since Julian is dead set on being Prime Minister of Australia, that is where we must reside."

It made wonderful sense. "I'm fine with that. But aren't you taking Olivia's and Bram's falling in with the plan a little bit for granted?"

"Not really. This is the kind of life they both want. I think they'll grab the opportunity with both hands. This house is big enough to shelter us all. It may turn out that Julian will renounce the baronetcy after I'm gone. Who knows? That's a decision he will have to make in the future. Peter may well become the sixth Baron Wynd ham. Meanwhile I intend to stick around for a very long time."

"And we may well have more children," Cate pointed out, a brilliant light in her eyes.

"You're planning on more children, then?" Ashe asked in a low, provocative voice.

"Well, we can *try*!" Cate laughed, her hand moving with great sensuous delight down over his superb body. "I love you. Love you. Love you," she cried. "My darling, my dearest, Ashe. I plan on telling you every day of our lives."

"And I'll be holding you to that!" Ashe promised. "Do you know I realise now, no matter past desolations, I've lived with the possibility of one day seeing you again," he admitted with wonderment.

"I did too." Cate sighed blissfully, thinking the great joys of the present were folding away all the unhappiness of the past. "What if we had missed one another?"

A hush fell over them at the thought. "We haven't. Fate has smiled on us." Ashe leaned down to kiss her, his love flowing like a benediction. "It's given us back our one true soul mate."

"And our son." Cate felt doubly blessed.

"I see a tiny bit of me in there?" He stared into her eyes, capturing his own image.

"A lot!'

"My father too," Ashe mused. "The way Julian talks it's as though my father has come alive."

"My father has come alive for me." Tears caught in Cate's eyes and throat. "He is such a fine man. He didn't know about me. Isn't that terrible?"

"Terrible indeed," Ashe confirmed with only the mildest irony.

"My mother and my aunt made sure of that. I wonder if Stella ever feels shame for the things she's done?"

"I'd be a tad astonished if she did," Ashe said dryly. "Stella obviously has the capacity for blotting away guilt and shame. Some people are like that. They can never admit to wrongdoing. It's always somebody else's fault if things turn out badly."

"The textbook narcissist?" Cate suggested quietly. "She was happy when there were only the three of us. She does love Jules."

"Until he rebelled," Ashe pointed out firmly. "No rebelling allowed. *You* were okay as long as you remained with no permanent partner in your life. Stella might have had to go then. She must have feared that."

"Well, now she's making a life of her own." Cate sighed. "I think Gerald deserves more. Or at least a warning. But the great thing is *I* have all of my men in my life. It's the way it was supposed to have happened. I suppose even destiny can sometimes get things wrong."

"Be grateful this time it's got it *right*!" Ashe said emphatically. "Are we, or are we not, the perfect match?"

Cate touched her fingers gently to his mouth. "You get your answer when you've made love to me again."

Love was a revelation. It was also a miracle when all the forces of the universe conspired to bring two people together.

These forces had various names. Fate, Destiny, Chance. Call it what you will.

* * * * *